700 X

## "SLIDE! SLIDE!

The pitcher checked Scrapper Mitchell on the bag at first, then delivered.

David "DT" Green's bat flashed around in a blur and made solid contact.

Off with the pitch, Scrapper raced around second and headed for third. The ball flew past the center fielder before he could even turn. Then it crashed against the center-field fence and bounded back.

Mitchell dug hard rounding third. The center fielder rifled the relay throw into the second baseman, who turned and gunned the ball toward home.

"Slide! *Slide!*" yelled Magic Ramirez from the Rosemont Rockets' dugout.

Fifteen feet from home, Scrapper lunged headfirst toward the plate. A cloud of dust whirled up, covering the whole home-plate area.

The crowd gasped and held its breath. Slowly the dust settled. *"Safe!"* the umpire cried.

**Other books in the ROOKIES series:**

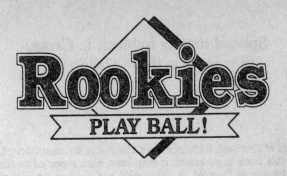

# Rookies
## PLAY BALL!

**Mark Freeman**

BALLANTINE BOOKS • NEW YORK

# Special thanks to Mark L. Crose.

Rookies

RLI: VL: 6 & up
     IL: 6 & up

Copyright © 1989 by the Jeffrey Weiss Group, Inc.

Produced by the Jeffrey Weiss Group, Inc.
133 Fifth Avenue
New York, New York 10003

All rights reserved under International and Pan-American Copyright Conventions. Published in the United States of America by Ballantine Books, a division of Random House, Inc., New York, and simultaneously in Canada by Random House of Canada Limited, Toronto.

Library of Congress Catalog Card Number: 88-92812

ISBN 0-345-35902-X

Printed in Canada

First Edition: June 1989

19  18  17  16  15  14

For my favorite rookies, Mathew and Michael.

# ROOKIES
## *Play Ball*

# ONE

Roberto "Magic" Ramirez stood on the pitcher's mound, staring down at the batter. The undisputed ace of the Rosemont High School baseball team, Roberto was in complete command. The sun's rays, breaking through the clouds, even seemed to spotlight him.

"Hey, batta, batta!" "Hum it in there, hum it in there!"

The infielders surrounding Roberto filled the air with their constant chatter. Roberto glanced around at them and smiled.

Stuffing the green tail of his jersey into his baseball pants, Roberto went into his windup. He unleashed the full fury of his whiplike arm and listened to the umpire's loud screech.

"Striiike one!"

The Washington High School batter never got his bat off his shoulder. Two more pitches came screaming in over the plate with the same results.

"Striiike three, you're outta there!" echoed through the park.

The Rosemont team let out a whoop and ran for the dugout. Checking out the scoreboard, Roberto saw a long string of zeroes. It was the bottom of the eighth of a scoreless game between Rosemont High and Washington, with Rosemont coming to bat.

Tension filled the air in this first-round game of the Illinois State high school baseball championships. But Roberto's sparkling pitching effort had filled his teammates with confidence.

Dropping down onto the hard wooden bench in the dugout, Roberto sat between his two best friends—Glen Mitchell and David Green.

The three of them had taken turns all year in leading their team to victory. There was no question that they were the stars of the team.

Glen, known as "Scrapper" to his teammates for his hot temper, punched Roberto on his left shoulder. "Nice work, Magic! We've got this thing wrapped up."

Taking off his cap and running his fingers through his wavy black hair, Roberto stared at his friend in amazement. "Don't ya think we could use a run or two before you get too excited?"

David Green stood up and grinned down at

his two friends. "No sweat, guys. Just leave that to me!" At six foot five, and a solid 195 pounds, people listened to the charismatic leader of the team. "C'mon, you guys," he shouted at the rest of the team, "Magic thinks we need a few runs. Let's go get 'em!"

Charged up, the Rosemont Rockets started cheering and clapping their hands. But despite their team leader's appeal, Rosemont's Charlie Neal, Thomas Brown, and Craig Whitcomb all were retired quickly in the bottom of the eighth—three up and three down.

Scooping up his glove, Roberto headed out to the mound, still trying to preserve a scoreless tie.

"Come on Robbie! You can do it!" Rosa Ramirez's voice carried out through the crowd noise and brought a smile to Roberto's face. His mother sat up in the stands behind the Rosemont bench with the entire family. They tried not to miss any of Roberto's pitching starts, and since the play-offs were now on, they would go to every game.

Since moving to the United States from the Dominican Republic four years earlier, the Ramirez family leaned heavily on each other for comfort and support. Roberto winked up at his mother when he heard her cheer.

The first Washington High batter in the top of the ninth worked hard to get on base. He fouled off five pitches before finally getting a base on balls.

Roberto cursed under his breath. Frustrated and angered, he tried to blow four pitches by the next batter and wound up walking him, too. Suddenly, there was an ominous hush over the Rosemont bench and the players out on the field.

The Rockets' coach, Tony La Russo, sprang out of the dugout and headed for the mound. He knew Roberto might be in trouble. He'd seen it before. Once Roberto started to walk a few batters, he was capable of completely losing his confidence.

Grabbing his young pitcher by the shoulder, La Russo gently shook him. "You okay, Ramirez?"

Roberto's gaze nervously searched out his family behind the dugout. He couldn't bring himself to answer.

"Listen, kid. You're just overthrowing the damn ball. Relax. You've been pitching super. Don't force it now, just let it happen." The coach's words didn't seem to make an impact.

La Russo stood for a moment staring at his ace pitcher, hoping he would snap out of his mood. He was about to take the ball from Ramirez's glove and signal for a reliever when Glen Mitchell loped over to the mound from second base.

Glen was a baseball man through and through. His father, Joe Mitchell, had been a former major-league star with the Philadelphia Phillies. Scrapper's knowledge and instincts for the game were a tremendous benefit to the team.

"Hey, Magic Man! What's going on?" Scrapper asked his friend.

Roberto turned and saw Glen's concern. He shrugged and kicked the dirt.

"Hey, guys"—the home plate umpire took two steps toward the mound—"let's play ball!"

Glen knew it was now or never. He reached over and pulled Roberto's green hat bill down over his eyes, trying to break the tension. "C'mon, Magic! Let's get this over with. The pizza's getting cold. Just hum a few down the middle and we'll do the rest!"

A broad smile slowly crept over Roberto's face. "You'd better, man, or I'll be all over you."

Waving as he walked back toward second, Glen taunted him, "Just pitch the ball. You'll see!"

Taking a deep breath, Roberto nodded his head. "I'm okay, Coach."

Hoping he was right, Coach La Russo nodded and walked back to the dugout.

The catcher flashed two fingers, signaling for a curve ball or "deuce." Roberto went into his stretch and delivered the pitch. It nibbled the outside corner of the plate, but the umpire called it a ball.

Frustrated, Roberto slammed his glove against his leg. He then grooved his next pitch right down the middle of the plate. Roberto saw the look in the batter's eyes and knew he had made a mistake.

The Washington High player took a ferocious cut and sent a shot singing at Roberto. Before he could even react, the ball was by him. But Glen got off toward second at the crack of the bat, dove, and speared the ball on its first hop at the edge of the outfield grass. Scrambling to his feet, he gunned it to the shortstop covering second, who then relayed to first for the double play.

"Unbelievable!"

"Fantastic!"

"Way to go, Mitchell!" The cheers rose up from the stands in appreciation for the spectacular play.

The fabulous twin killing had prevented a sure run. The Washington team still had a runner on third, but now there were two outs.

Roberto turned toward his friend at second.

Glen threw a fist into the air and yelled, "I told ya! You pitch 'em, we'll get 'em!"

Inspired by Glen's resolve, Roberto hurled three pitches past the next batter.

"Striiike three!" the umpire called, ending the top of the ninth.

Roberto wiped the sweat from his brow and checked the scoreboard again. "Bottom of the ninth . . . still no score!"

David Green ran into the dugout from center field and slammed his glove against the wall. The dust flew up in a cloud as the mitt flopped to the ground. He searched out his batting helmet and then grabbed his favorite thirty-three–ounce bat. He was batting cleanup.

Glen, batting third in the inning, moved up and down the bench, urging his teammates to victory. "C'mon, you guys, let's fire up a little out there. All we need is one. All we need is one!"

Bill Wiley, Washington High's pitcher, was determined to hold the Rockets. He struck out the first batter and got the second one to tap back weakly to the mound. No one had hit the ball out of the infield since the second inning.

It was Glen Mitchell's turn. He advanced from the on-deck circle toward home, and his eyes focused on the left field fence. His gaze never moved from the area deep in the gap between left and center.

The Washington infielders yelled encouragement to their pitcher. "This guy's gonna try and end it all. Keep it down, keep it down."

Glen stood in at the plate and took several vicious practice swings. He reached down and grabbed a handful of dirt and rubbed it into his hands. His eyes took one more glance out to the wall and then focused on the pitcher.

On the first pitch, Glen squared around and laid a perfect bunt down the third-base line. Caught flat-footed, the Washington third baseman never had a chance. Glen easily beat out the throw and was on with a single.

"Atta way, Scrapper! Wayda go, wayda go!"

Coach La Russo led the cheers from the Rosemont dugout.

The next batter marched toward the plate with a gleam in his eye. David Green was pumped and ready. He dug into the batter's box with his cleats. The Washington pitcher stared at him with contempt.

Washington's catcher glanced up at David. He recognized him and ran out to the mound to talk to his pitcher.

"Don't let this guy beat you, Bill. Pitch him carefully."

"He hasn't hit me yet, has he?" Washington's pitcher said.

"Hey, this guy's good. He leads the state in home runs this year. They don't call him 'Downtown' for nothing."

"Yeah, I know. But Mr. DT hasn't done anything but pop up against me. I can take him." Wiley's cockiness scared the catcher.

"Just throw him junk. Don't give him anything he can hit!"

The pitcher just smiled. "I can blow this ball right by him on the outside corner. You watch. He won't be able to touch it."

When the catcher returned behind the plate, David smashed his bat down hard on the white rubber base. The catcher became more nervous.

After several signals for curves and change-ups, all shaken off, the Washington catcher gave his pitcher what he'd been waiting for . . . the sign for a fastball. He set up on the outside corner of the plate.

David waited. He knew by the look on the pitcher's face that he was going to give him the pitch he needed.

The pitcher went into the stretch, checked Glen as he danced on and off the bag at first, and then delivered.

David's bat flashed around in a blur and made perfect contact with the pitch. The ball took off like a cannon shot straightaway toward center.

Off with the pitch, Glen raced around second and headed for third. The ball flew past the center fielder before he could even turn. When it crashed against the center-field fence and bounded back toward the outfielder, everyone knew there was going to be a play at the plate . . . and it was going to be close.

Glen dug hard rounding third, never hesitating or looking for a signal from the third-base coach. His mind had been set when he heard the bat make contact.

The center fielder rifled the relay throw into the second baseman, who then turned and gunned the ball toward home.

"Slide! Slide!" The bleachers were thundering from the pounding feet of the Rosemont fans.

The Washington fans were screaming, "Throw him out! Gun him down!"

Fifteen feet from home, Glen lunged headfirst toward the plate. A cloud of dust whirled up, covering the whole home-plate area.

The crowd gasped and held its breath. Slowly the dust settled. The umpire's hands spread down and away as he screamed out, "Safe!"

The Rosemont team erupted from the dugout, cheering and waving. They circled around Glen and mobbed nim as he struggled to get back on his feet. David came running in from second, found Glen, lifted him to his feet, and offered him the highest high-five ever attempted.

"Wayda go, Scraps!" David yelled over the crowd noise.

Jumping as high as he could, Glen found David's hand with his. "No problem, DT! No problem!"

David looked down at him and laughed. "Yeah. There wouldn't have been . . . except you run like a duck!"

Glen belted him in the shoulder. Wiping the dirt from his uniform, Glen had a broad smile across his face.

As the mob scene drifted toward the sidelines, Roberto struggled to his two friends and wrapped his arms around their shoulders. "Great job, guys. But next time, do ya think you could back me up with a few more runs? I pitch real well with a five-run lead, ya know."

Glen knocked Roberto's hat off and laughed. "How would you know? You never had one!"

In the locker room , Coach La Russo called his team together. "Great game, guys. You all played super ball."

The locker room broke out in loud cheers. "Yeah! All the way! All right!"

"But . . ." La Russo's voice turned down in volume. ". . . I just got word on who won the other game in our bracket. Our semifinal opponent's going to be Central Valley!"

The team let out a collective roar. Everyone knew Central was the defending state champion . . . and the team that eliminated Rosemont in the play-offs last year.

La Russo pulled himself up to his full five-foot-six-inch height. His players seemed to tower above him. "They're a good team. And we all know about last year . . . they kicked everyone's butt—including ours. So we can count on one thing for sure. They're not going to give up that state title without a fight."

David Green jumped up on the bench and looked out over all his teammates. His blue eyes sparkled. "Yeah! And we're gonna give them one, Coach. Right, guys!"

"Right!" the rest of the Rockets cheered, throwing towels and mitts in the air.

# TWO

Roberto Ramirez stretched lazily on his bed and tried to open his eyes. The tantalizing aroma of sizzling bacon brought his senses closer to full attention. Slowly but surely, he started to realize it must be time to get up.

His mother's voice finally broke through the last veil of morning slumber. "Robbie! You're going to be late for school. Hurry."

Groaning, Roberto tossed back the covers, raced through the shower, and threw on his clothes. In ten minutes he was down in the kitchen.

"Morning, Mom . . . Dad. Sorry I'm late," he said as he sat down at the breakfast table.

His father, Carlos, looked up from his morning paper. "I see you got another letter in the mail. . . . What school was it . . . some Big Ten school, wasn't it? . . . Northwestern or . . .?"

"Michigan, Dad. They've got a good pre-med program there and . . ."

"And a good baseball team?" his mother added.

Roberto smiled. It had been his dream since boyhood to become a doctor. But since moving to the United States, his love for baseball had consumed much of his time.

"Yes, Mom. They might even offer me a scholarship. At least that's what Coach La Russo told me."

"That would be excellent, Robbie. You know, we are very proud of all you have done." Rosa Ramirez continued cooking while she talked. "I'm sure Michigan is a very fine school."

Carlos rose from the table and gathered his briefcase and suit coat. He turned to Roberto. "If baseball can help you obtain your goals, that's great. But make sure you choose a school with the right goal in mind."

"Sure, Dad." Roberto's eyes sought relief from the penetrating stare of his father. "See you tonight."

Roberto gulped the last bit of his orange juice just as his dad walked out the door. "I've got to run, too, Mom. The coach told us never to be late for school. As varsity players, we've got to set good examples."

Rosa smiled and gave her son a kiss on the

forehead. "I'm sure you do, Robbie. Your coach is a good man."

Grabbing his books, Roberto flew out the door and raced toward school. "'Bye, Mom. Catch you later."


The walk to school was a short one and provided Roberto just enough time to collect his thoughts before the school day. It was a beautiful spring morning in the Chicago suburb of Rosemont. The sky was crystal clear, unlike the hazy, hot days of summer, and it made Roberto anxious to get back on the mound.

Roberto pulled up the collar of his varsity sweater. It was white and sported a big green R with three baseball symbols. He always wore it after important games.

Entering the main hallway at Rosemont High, Roberto checked the clock in the office and saw he was in good shape. He walked past the first row of gray steel lockers and ran into a crowd of people surrounding his friend DT Green. They were all slapping him on the back and congratulating him on his game-winning hit of the day before.

The voices in the circle of students rang out with praise. "What a shot! As soon as you connected, man, I knew it was over for Washington."

"Yeah, me, too," another kid answered. "And you should have seen the look on the face of their wimp pitcher. Man, did he ever look sick!"

David stopped them short. "Hey, you got to give him credit for trying. He really pitched a pretty good game against us."

One of the students caught sight of Roberto. "Speaking of good . . ."

"Hey, there he is. Our main man!"

David turned and saw his friend Roberto. "Magic! What's happening?"

The two bumped forearms together, a team ritual, and Roberto said, "I woulda liked that game a lot more if that ball had cleared the fence. But, hey, if that's the best you can do . . ."

The small crowd surrounding the two baseball players broke out in laughter.

Glen Mitchell turned the corner at the other end of the long Rosemont hallway and headed for his homeroom. He caught the tail end of the exchange between his teammates and laughed. "And this guy," David said," if he could run with one foot in front of the other like a normal person, that play wouldn't even have been close. I've seen slugs with a bigger head of steam."

"Cut me, man . . . cut me. I'm dying." Glen pretended to double over in pain.

The piercing sound of the first bell rang through the hallway, stopping their conversation. It signaled a two-minute warning before the first class.

"Uh-oh! We better get going, guys. Talk to you

later," said David. A leader on and off the field, he had a positive impact on everyone who knew him.

Glen looked over his shoulder as he headed down the hall. "You guys still coming over tomorrow night to watch the game?"

Roberto waved. "You got it."

But David's shoulders slumped as he let out a groan. "Sorry, men. I forgot I've got to work tonight. Ol' man Phifer wants us to take an inventory at the store. I can't get out of it."

"Tough break," Glen said. "We'll catch you later, then."

As a reminder to his teammates, David hollered back through the noisy, crowded hallway, "Beat Central!"

After school ended, David, Roberto, and Glen all headed for the Mitchell house as they usually did on off days. The boys entered the house and descended on the kitchen like a swarm of locusts. Loaded with plates full of snacks, they went down three steps from the kitchen into the sunken family room and sprawled out to relax.

The family room in the home was filled with trophies, plaques, autographed balls, special bats, and articles of clothing from Joe Mitchell's years in professional baseball. For twelve years he led the nomadic life of a professional ballplayer . . . traveling and playing all around the country. Now he was the regional sales manager for a national sporting-goods manufacturer.

"You guys know Central Valley really is gonna be tough," Glen said as he washed down a chocolate-chip cookie with a huge gulp of milk. "I sure wish you were pitching, Magic!"

"Hey, Brian's going to do just fine. We just have to do a better job of getting some runs for him."

David agreed. "But they've got a lot of fire-power on that team. They've gotta be averaging about eight or nine runs a game."

"Yeah, and a bunch of home runs," said Glen. "And, we've got to find some way to shut down their big gun. . . . What's his name? . . ."

"Williams . . . Jason Williams." The name was easy for Roberto to recall.

Glen's memory came to life. "Yeah, I remember. He's the guy who launched that rocket off you last year in the play-offs. That thing's probably still circling the earth."

"Geez, it wasn't that bad. It just barely cleared the fence. . . ."

"Yeah? Whose fence? None of us ever saw it come down!" said Glen.

"Anything that travels that far oughta have a stewardess on it," David added.

Everybody broke up.

Dave bit into an apple. "Anyway, we have to forget last year. It's Wednesday's game that counts now. We're not gonna let them get away from us this year. All we've got to do is beat

Central Valley, and then 'Fireball' Ramirez here can wrap up the championship game . . . right?"

Roberto gave him a thumbs-up.

"We don't want to let down those scouts, do we?" Glen asked.

"Scouts?" Roberto was surprised. "You mean, Central Valley has sent scouts up here?"

David and Glen groaned in unison. "C'mon. Where've you been? We've had major-league scouts show up for our last three games," said David.

"Are you kidding me?" Roberto dropped his cupcake. He was stunned. He'd spent all of his time worrying about college. The thought of a career in major-league baseball had apparently never crossed his mind.

David shook his head. "Geez, you really must be in a fog when you're on the mound. Haven't you seen those guys up in the bleachers with the radar gun, charting every pitch you throw, clocking us when we run around the bases?"

"Heck no! I never saw a thing. Why didn't you guys tell me? When did you find out?"

Glen grabbed another cookie. "I thought you knew all about it. The Coach said they've talked to him about several players on the team, but he wouldn't say any more."

Roberto's mind clicked into gear.

"You say they were charting pitches during my last game?"

Glen couldn't resist. "Yeah, they were check-

ing on that guy on the Washington team to see if
he could hit an easy curve ball."

"Funny. Very funny." Roberto leaned back and
crossed his hands behind his head. "I'll bet they
were checking out how I stood up under the
pressure of having no defense behind me while
I pitched."

David jumped up and flexed his muscles in
front of the mirrored trophy-display case. "I
hear they're always looking for left-handed
power hitters."

"Hey, that's just like our team. We need a
left-handed power hitter, too," said Glen. He
dodged just in time as the sofa pillow David
threw went whizzing by.

David turned serious again. "Well, one thing's
for certain. If we had scouts at our last few
games, there's going to be even more at the
Central Valley game. That team is loaded with
talent."

Roberto nodded. "Yeah. The last few years it's
been like they were a farm club for the Cubs.
What is there . . . three guys on the Cubbies
who used to be at Central?"

"Right . . . and about three more on this
year's team that will probably make it. At least
that's what my dad told me," said Glen.

"He oughta know," David claimed.

Glen's face scrunched up in a scowl and he
shook his head. "Yeah, well, it's been awhile
since he played. Things have changed."

"Not at Central Valley," said David. "Those big

farm boys from downstate still know how to hit the ball a mile. That Williams guy can hit an aspirin tablet at night!"

"We just have to make sure he hits it at someone . . . right?"

Roberto lifted his dirty sneakers off the coffee table when he noticed Glen's dad walk into the room.

"Hi, boys. What's going on?" Joe Mitchell's sudden appearance immediately changed the mood of the group. A solid five foot ten in height, and still at his playing weight of 170 pounds, he somehow seemed larger than life to Roberto and David. His dark hair was starting to gray, but he still looked ready to play at a moment's notice.

"We were just talking about playing Central Valley," David said. "This year we're gonna be ready."

Joe looked at each boy and nodded his head. "I hope so. That was pretty embarrassing last year. We'd better get a few more hits this time."

Glen rolled his eyes. He curled his fingers into a fist and started to bounce his hand against the armrest of the couch. His dad's gaze leveled on him.

"I hope you've been working on getting up in the batter's box, son. I've told you a dozen times you're laying back too deep. You need to be more aggressive up there at the plate."

Glen's dad stood up and assumed a batting stance.

"And cock that right elbow back like this," he lectured.

Roberto and David watched the steam rising in their friend's face. They knew they'd better change the subject.

"Hey, Mr. Mitchell"—Roberto pointed at a ball in the trophy case— "isn't that autograph Pete Rose's?"

"Yep. Now there's a man who flat understood what hitting was all about. I've got some old exhibition-game tapes you should take a look at sometime, Glen."

"Great, Dad." Glen stood up and started walking toward the kitchen.

"I'm not through talking to you, son," Joe called out.

"Sorry, Dad." Glen motioned to his two friends when his father wasn't looking. "We've all got to get going. We're meeting a couple of other guys from the team."

Joe sat down in his recliner. He looked at his son sceptically. "Well. This can wait until you get back. It's something you've got to start working on, though. Old habits are hard to break."

Waving him off, Glen walked through the kitchen and out of the house, followed by his two teammates. Once safely outside, he blew off the tension that had been building.

"Geez, I wish he'd just cut me some slack."

"C'mon, Scrap. Don't ya think you're being a little hard on your old man? He's just trying to help you." David rested a hand on Glen's shoulder.

Roberto chimed in, "Yeah. And ya gotta admit he does have a lot of valuable experience. It's not like some dads who don't even know what they're talking about."

Glen stared off into the distance. Annoyed with his two friends, he fought back the urge to argue with them. He knew it wouldn't do any good.

"Okay, you two jerks." Glen smacked his teammates on the back. "I'll have him come to practice and help you with *your* games."

"No, thanks," David said, stopping short and getting into a boxing stance. "We got enough trouble with one Mitchell already!"

# THREE

The Rosemont High School gymnasium was jammed to the rafters with kids. A muffled roar echoed through the building as a thousand conversations filled the air. Brightly colored posters hung from the walls with slogans like: Destroy Central! and Rockets Bomb Central Valley! Everyone was ready for the big game.

The pep rally started with the screeching blare of feedback from the microphone. It acted as a signal to everyone that the show was about to begin. A restless quiet took over the crowd.

As the lights dimmed, the baseball team came crashing through the gym doors. They ran up on the makeshift stage and stood waving. The student body burst into applause and cheers.

In their white skirts and kelly green rally

sweaters, the cheerleading squad came somer-saulting out in front of the students. They clapped and started the chant, "Beat Central! Beat Central! Beat Central!"

The crowd stamped their feet and screamed. The building started to shake.

"I wonder what's going to happen if we win," Roberto asked David as he poked an elbow in his ribs.

"*When!* It's *when* we win, dummy, not *if.* . . . I don't know, but I'll bet it'll be cool."

David shifted his weight from one foot to the other as he became more and more uncomfortable waiting for the chance to sit down.

The rally squad was singing: "Who's the team that is the best? R–O–C–K–E–T–S! Rockets!"

When the chanting and cheering subsided, the Rockets' coach stepped up to the microphone. "Thank you very much for that tremendous reception. It means a lot to the ballplayers and to me." He paused to wipe the perspiration from his forehead.

"This team sat down in January and talked about last year. We had a great season . . . far better than anyone else expected. We won the league championship. We even won the regional tournament." The crowd cheered. He waited for the crowd to quiet down. "But one thing didn't sit well with us."

The crowd started to chant again. "Beat Central! Beat Central!"

Coach La Russo raised his hands and silenced

the students. "Maybe we weren't ready for a team like Central Valley last year . . . but we're ready now."

A low roar grew in the corners of the gym.

"Tomorrow we make it happen. Tomorrow . . . we beat Central!"

The student body exploded in cheers. The foot stomping and chanting rose to earsplitting heights. "Beat Central! Beat Central! Beat Central!"

Roberto felt the goose bumps tingling up and down his back. The team started clapping to the beat as they filed out of the rally. The players picked up the chant. "Beat Central! Beat Central!"

Leaving the gym, the players entered the main hallway back toward school. They broke up into small groups as well-wishers and friends sought them out to encourage them. Glen, David, and Roberto stood to one side of the huge hallway, right in front of the science lab.

Roberto's eyes were still wide with excitement. "Boy, that was really something!"

"Yeah." David took off his letterman jacket because of the heat. "Coach really got 'em worked up in there, didn't he? I think we gotta win this game!"

Glen nodded. "Yeah. Or we're big trouble."

"You already are, Mitchell. Nothing's gonna change that." The scornful remark was heard by all three boys.

Whipping around, Glen searched for the antagonist. "Who said that?"

Four boys were walking down the center of the hall. The one in the middle, a blond-haired boy with a crew cut and menacing dark eyes, spat out a reply. "You think you're so-o-o cool up on that stage. But you're nothing, man. Nothing but a wimp with an old man who won't quit making you look good."

Before his friends knew it, Glen was on the boy. Both fists flailing away, Scrapper was living up to his reputation.

Fighting back their urge to join him, David and Roberto pulled Glen off the heckler.

"C'mon, Glen. He isn't worth it!" David struggled to lift his friend to his feet.

Scrapper wouldn't quit. "I'm gonna shut this geek's mouth up once and for all! He's been on me all year."

"So what?" Roberto got an armlock on Glen. "Let him go. We can't afford to have you suspended for fighting. That's what he wants. Geez, don't let him win."

Glen struggled to gain control of his temper. He knew what Roberto said was true. Kneeling over his enemy, he growled, "Don't show your face around me again unless you want it smashed. Got it?"

"I don't get anything from you. But you're gonna get yours someday, jerk."

"It won't be from you if I do, dipstick." Curling his hand back into a fist, Glen continued, "And if you want some more of this, meet me after school out by the ball field."

"Fat chance, ya dumb jock."

Glen was about to pounce on him again, but Roberto grabbed his arm as he spotted a teacher rounding the corner of the hallway.

"Cool it, Glen. This isn't the right time."

Pointing his finger, Glen swore in a low voice, "Someday . . . just you 'n me, man."

David stood between them and motioned for everyone to leave. "Show's over, everybody. Move it. Move it!" He then wheeled toward his friends. "Let's get outta here before anything else goes wrong. I can't believe you, Mitchell."

He continued to mumble under his breath as he led his two friends away from the scene. "The day before the biggest game of our season. What's the matter with you, Mitchell? Don't let those kinda guys bother you. We've got to concentrate on the game."

Rubbing his sore knuckles, Glen nodded. "I know it. I know it. I don't know why I let that happen."

Roberto smacked him in the back of the head. "Just don't let it happen again, that's all!"

Glen continued to rub knuckles on his sore hand. "Okay, man. Okay!"


As Glen, Roberto, and David walked out onto the baseball field after school for practice, Coach La Russo spotted them and waved them over to the sidelines. The look on his face made them very uneasy.

David pulled at his green warm-up jacket and tried to lighten the mood. With a big smile he said, "Great speech today, Coach. You really got everyone fired up with that one."

La Russo's expression didn't change. "What's the matter with you guys?"

David continued to act as spokesman for the trio. "Nothing, Coach. In fact, we were just saying—"

"Cut it, Green." La Russo stared at Glen. "I saw that fight in the hallway today, Mitchell. What was that all about?"

Glen jumped to attention. "Hey, Coach, some guy was bad-mouthing us and the rest of the team, and I let him have it."

"You let him have it? Great," La Russo shouted, "And what would have happened if some other teacher had seen that fight? You know where you'd be right now? Sitting in Mr. Morris's office, waiting to hear how long you're suspended. Get the picture, Mitchell?"

"Yeah." Glen hung his head and mumbled.

"I didn't hear you."

"Yes, sir. I'm sorry."

Roberto stood silently, but David again tried to break the mood. "It won't happen again, Coach. We'll just go out and start practice, if that's okay."

"No, that's not okay. Now, I want to know what's going on. What's really bothering you guys? I saw it in the last few games. All of you were off . . . unsure of yourselves. Taking that extra split second to make sure rather than just reacting."

Roberto finally spoke up. He pushed back his cap and let out a sigh. "There's been a lot of pressure lately, Coach."

La Russo looked puzzled. "This game's never bothered you guys before. You've always played for fun. That's the way it should be."

Roberto continued. "But now there's more. Reporters, college recruiters, even—" He couldn't say the words.

"What?" Their coach looked confused.

Glen finished the thought. "Major-league scouts, Coach. We've seen 'em up in the stands."

"So that's it." La Russo chuckled out loud.

"Coach, all that stuff is important. We're talking about our whole future," David said.

"I understand. I'm not laughing at you. I'm laughing because I should have known and done something about it. Now listen, guys. You've been outstanding ballplayers for me for three years now. There isn't a major college in the area and probably half the country that doesn't know about you. But major-league or college scouts don't make their decisions based on one or two games. They know your career stats already. They'd only be here now to see if you've got the right attitude out on the field . . . and off."

"How would they know about that?" asked Glen.

"Well, they're going to talk to me, for starters, and probably anyone else who knows you, and try to get a feel for that. Then they'll want to briefly meet you and talk to you. That's how they'll do it."

"What if we look bad out in the field, though? Won't that kill our chances?" David asked.

"Look, guys. Like I said, you've got your whole career as a reference. I was a scout for a good many years, and let me tell you . . . my guess is that any scout interested in any of you has probably already made up his mind. One game isn't going to change it. So if I were you, I'd just relax and go out and play good ball. This is either your last or second-to-last game in high school. You might as well enjoy them."

The boys looked at each other and nodded. The realization was hitting them hard again. Their high-school careers were just about over.

David put his hand on Coach La Russo's shoulder. "Thanks, Coach."

La Russo chuckled again. "Okay, enough talking. Now, hustle your butts onto the field and let's play some ball."

"All right!" Glen, David, and Roberto rang out in unison as they ran out on the field.

# FOUR

Glen Mitchell sat in his family room, absently staring at his father's trophy case. He thought about how many hours he had spent in that very room with his friends and yet never noticed some of the things in it. *An amazing assortment of junk,* he thought as he shook his head.

His father's years in professional baseball seemed a long time ago to Glen now. He almost never thought about them. Only when his friends were with him in this room did the significance of all the memorabilia hit him.

He shoveled another handful of potato chips into his mouth and washed them down with a swig of Coke. Reaching for the television remote control, he was surprised by his father's entrance into the room.

"Hi, pal," Joe Mitchell greeted his son.

"Yo, Dad. What's up?"

"That's what I thought I'd find out from you. We never finished our talk the other day. You been working on changing that stance at practice yet?"

"Coach La Russo doesn't think I need to change. He says I'm doing just fine."

Joe Mitchell threw up his hands. "Well, if you don't want my help . . . if you'd rather trust someone like La Russo who's never amounted to anything in the game . . ."

Glen turned away and looked out the window. "I think he's done okay. Playing professionally isn't the only way to learn about the game."

Joe sat down in the recliner directly opposite his son. "Yes, it is. It gives a man a whole new outlook on life. You see things differently when you know you're the very best at what you do. And I hope you discover that someday."

"I'll do fine."

"Yeah. Well, not if you don't start listening to the people who can help you. Even if it means listening to your own father once in a while."

Fighting back his emotions, Glen couldn't look his father in the eye. "I do, Dad. Just don't worry about my game too much."

Joe Mitchell felt the ice in his son's words. "Worry isn't the right word. I care . . . that's what I'm trying to say."

Glen got up. "Yeah, Dad, I know. Look, I gotta meet the guys down at Eat."

Joe Mitchell nodded as he watched his son leave the room. His head slumped into his chest. "Yeah, sure. Go ahead and go. I'll show you what I mean about the stance later."

He listened as the front door slammed shut.


Eat Burger, the favorite hangout of the Rosemont High School crowd, was packed. Even at nine o'clock on a week night it was hard to find a place to sit.

It was a stark white, old-fashioned diner with bright lights, big tables, a juke box, and the best burgers and shakes in town.

Glen found his two friends in a front booth, a crowd of people milling around their table. "Hey, guys, what's happening?"

Carrie Hall sat across the aisle from the three baseball players. Her luscious blue eyes were riveted on Glen. When he glanced her way, she blushed and flipped her long blond hair over her shoulder as she turned back to her girl friends.

"Whooh," Glen whistled through his teeth and shook his head.

"Park it here, Scraps. We've been waiting for you. Unless you have somewhere else you'd like to sit?" David teased as he looked over at Carrie.

"I wish," he sighed as he dropped down in the seat.

"What took you so long?" David asked.

"I decided to walk."

"Whoa." Roberto leaned back against the white, wooden bench. "You walked all the way from your house?"

"Yeah. I didn't feel like asking my dad for the car tonight. Mom was out with some bridge group, so I had no other choice."

"You coulda called one of us," Roberto said.

"Like I said . . . I decided to walk." Glen pulled his coat off and flung it next to him on the bench. A hat came flying across the diner at him. Glen caught it without a second thought and continued its flight away from its rightful owner.

David noticed the edge in Glen's voice. "Is something bothering you? You seem uptight."

Glen didn't want to get into his feelings about his father with his friends. He wasn't sure he understood them himself. He just shook his head. "Naw. I'm fine. Just a little tired. Probably jacked up about the game tomorrow. You know how it goes."

Roberto and David nodded but sensed that something else was up. They chose to ignore his obvious foul mood.

David blew his straw wrapper at Glen. "Aren't you gonna ask our boy wonder here why he's so happy? Or haven't you noticed the sheep-eating grin on the wolf?"

Glen sat up straight and looked at Roberto. "What's up?"

Puffing out his cheeks, Roberto gave his best

impression of a kazoo blowing out the Michigan fight song.

Glen caught on right away. "Michigan got a hold of you?"

"Well . . . not exactly, yet. But Coach La Russo told me they were going to."

Glen leaned across the table and bumped forearms with Roberto. "That's terrific, Magic. A scholarship to Michigan . . . that's big time, really big time!"

Roberto nodded. "Hey, man. Nothing's happened yet."

"It will. Trust me." Glen moved forward to the edge of his seat.

David stared off into space and daydreamed outloud, "Ohio State, Purdue, Indiana . . . what a conference. The Big Ten is really great. Football games in the fall, basketball in the winter . . . Geez . . . maybe Bobby Knight will throw a chair at you."

Roberto let out a sigh and nodded his head. Caught up in the excitement, he said, "Yeah, we'd have a blast there."

Glen and David let his comment pass. Instead they lifted their arms off the table as the waitress stopped by with their order.

"Here you go, guys. Enjoy!" Lilian had been a waitress at Eat Burger as long as the boys had been coming there. It was a toss-up over who had served the boys more meals . . . their mothers or Lilian.

"Thanks, Lilian. It looks terrific." David's eyes

lit up when he saw the burgers. But he was the only one who seemed hungry.

As he slurped down his chocolate shake, David poked Glen in the ribs. "Hey, what's the matter? I ordered that burg' just the way you like—burned."

Glen slid the plate over toward his friend. "It's all yours."

"No, man, I don't want your food. I just want to know what's bugging you."

"I guess I'm just all screwed up. I don't know what I'm doing." Glen flopped back against the bench. "It all seemed so clear. As long as we've been working together all season, trying to win the championship, I knew exactly what I was doing. As we get closer to that . . . I don't know . . . I feel kinda lost. I don't know what's next."

"Hey, you're not alone, Mitchell," David said. "But one thing you can do is pass me the ketchup."

Glen pushed the red bottle toward David and pointed toward Roberto. "Now, Magic here has it all figured out. He's gonna go to Michigan, get into medicine, and do something worthwhile with his life. Not to mention have a Jaguar and a condo in Hawaii by the time he's twenty-six."

Roberto threw his wadded-up napkin at Glen.

"Me, I don't know if I'm coming or going. I don't know what I want to do."

David stuck his hands up behind his head and wiggled them. "Hey, what about 'Cal State Disneyland'? You've always said every weekend Mickey'd be waiting for you."

A weak smile played on Glen's lips.

Roberto broke into song. "M–I–C–K–E–Y. . ."

All three boys laughed at Roberto's horrendous singing.

"C'mon, Glen, lighten up. You don't have to know what the heck you're gonna be today. Whadya think college is for, anyway?" David said. "If I go to Clairmont Community, who knows what I'll end up doing."

"Yeah," Roberto added. "Sometimes I'm not so sure if being a doctor is the right thing for me."

"Ah, c'mon. That's all you've ever talked about as long as we've known you," said Glen.

"Who else could sit through chemistry class and actually learn what all those positive ions and negative whatevers really meant?" asked David.

"Yeah, well sometimes I don't know. I can't really remember if it's been *my* dream or my family's. I just don't know," Roberto said.

Lilian walked over to the three boys after delivering some banana splits to the table next to them. "Why the long faces, guys? This doesn't look like the group that's celebrating a big win and getting ready for the state championships to me."

David swallowed and shrugged. "These guys are just weird, Lilian."

Lilian flashed her famous smile. "Well, just

don't tell me it's the food. I don't want to hear about it if there's problems with the food."

"Never," Roberto said, spearing an onion ring from his plate and taking a bite. "We just found out that there's more to life than playing baseball."

"Oh, huh!" Glen sneered, followed by a laugh. "Let's not go that far."

Lilian shook her head. "You kids kill me. I'm gonna miss you." Taking an empty plate from the table, she walked off toward the kitchen.

"You know, she's right. It's really ending."

Roberto stared at him. "Whaddaya mean?"

"Figure it out," David said. "School's out for us in three weeks. If you go to Michigan, if Glen goes to Cal State, and I go to Clairmont . . . well, we won't be seeing much of each other anymore."

The group sat silently for a minute.

Finally Roberto broke the spell. "No. It doesn't have to be that way. Just because we go to different schools doesn't mean we can't still be friends. We can stay in touch. We'll still be coming home here for all the holidays and stuff. There's no reason it has to end."

David put his hand out over the table. "I agree!"

One by one, Glen and Roberto followed.

"Hey, just like those guys on the Denver Broncos," Roberto said, "the Three Amigos!"

"Yeah. One for all and all for one," David said.

"That's the Three Musketeers, bozo. Even I know that much," growled Glen.

David shrugged him off. "Whatever. The important thing is that we aren't going to give up what we've got."

A feeling of relief settled over all three boys.

"Hey, where's my burg?" asked Glen.

Roberto laughed. "I think the human vacuum cleaner's already sucked it up."

David raised his hand and waved. "Lilian . . . I think we need help at this table."

Turning her head toward them, she laughed when she saw the positive change in their moods. "Boy, do you ever . . . And I mean lots of help!"

# FIVE

Rosemont High's bright yellow team bus pulled into Central Valley's parking lot along with two spirit buses. The three-hour trip from Chicago had started in high spirits for the Rockets baseball team. But now, silence stilled the air as nervous eyes peered from the windows, anxiously searching out the enemy. The tension inside the bus was stifling.

David, the team captain, led his teammates down the steps of the bus and into the warm afternoon sunshine. Squinting from the brightness, he looked around for the entrance of the gymnasium and the visitors' locker room.

"This way, guys," he called out as he spotted a welcoming sign. It was a picture of their Rocket mascot with a noose around its neck.

"Looks like they feel the same way about us as we do about them," Roberto said.

Glen felt the hairs on the back of his neck stand on end. "We'll just see who walks out of here alive. They're in for a shocker if they expect the same team they played last year!"

Filing into the locker room, the Rockets threw their bags down in front of the wooden benches and sat down. The team dressed silently.

Roberto pulled his green stirrup hose up over his white sanitaries knowing that he wouldn't see any action today unless there was an emergency. His arm needed the rest. The thought that this might be his last game for Rosemont kept edging into his mind.

Dressed and ready to go, Glen, tossed a ball against the wall. The sound of the horsehide crashing against the plaster and wood echoed through the locker room in a constant, rhythmic beat.

Coach La Russo paced the floor. His metal cleats scraping against the concrete moved in unison to Glen's bouncing ball.

At precisely four-thirty, Coach La Russo yelled, "Our time to practice . . . Let's do it, guys!"

The Rockets took the field and started their usual pregame warm-up drills. Standing next to David, Glen watched the Central Valley team staring at them from their dugout. "Look at those guys, DT."

"Yeah, what about 'em?"

"Losers, man."

David shoved his friend in the side. "I hear you," he said, and started to clap his hands together slowly, methodically. Glen joined in. Roberto, doing his stretching exercises with the other pitchers, saw his friends and followed their lead. Others picked up the rhythm and soon the whole team was clapping. Faster and faster it went, until the air was filled with a sound like machine-gun fire.

Coach La Russo felt goose bumps work their way down his back. "Okay, you guys. Come on in. We're ready!"

As visiting team, Rosemont was the first to bat. They watched as Central Valley, clad in their red-and-gray uniforms, took the field.

Glen looked out from the dugout at them. "Man, those guys are huge. Look at that first baseman. He should be playing for the Chicago Bears."

"*That's* Jason Williams," Roberto reminded his friends.

"Move over, Refrigerator!" quipped David.

"I know how I'd pitch that guy this year," said Roberto. "Outside. Way outside. When he gets a hold of one . . . look out!" Shaking his head, Roberto just walked up and down the dugout.

When Bobby Judson drew a lead-off walk for the Rockets, the dugout exploded in cheers from the Rosemont fans. But the next two batters flew out and struck out.

David Green stepped up to the plate.

The Central Valley pitcher had done his homework and pitched David very carefully. He kept his off-speed pitches high and away from David and worked the count to three balls and one strike. Rather than walk David, the pitcher tried to sneak one pitch in on the inside corner of the plate.

The crack of the bat froze the Central Valley right fielder for a split second as he tried to judge the flight of the ball. By the time he took off for it, there was no catching up. The ball bounced and rolled into the deep right corner of the outfield.

Racing around the bases, Bobby scored from first. By the time the relay came in to the infield, David stood on third with a stand-up triple. Rosemont was ahead 1–0.

The Rockets let out a roar. "Way to go, DT! All right! All right! Let's keep it going!"

Unfortunately, a strikeout ended the inning.

Central Valley was retired in their half of the first inning, and the game settled down to a defensive struggle. Rosemont's Brian Holmes and Central's Keith Russell kept the hits to a minimum, and there were no additional runs. Entering the fifth inning, the score was still 1–0.

In the bottom of the fifth, a lead-off walk gave Central the start of something. The next two batters popped out. Central Valley's first baseman, Jason Williams, lumbered toward the plate.

Working carefully against the gigantic batter, Brian ran the count to two and two. Coach La Russo called out to the mound, "Atta way, Holmes, atta way. Keep it down."

Brian nodded. He went into the stretch and threw a low fastball that was out of the strike zone. But Williams liked it, anyway. With a ferocious cut that resembled a golf swing, the first baseman caught the pitch on the fat part of the bat and sent out a screaming line drive. It was still rising when it cleared the left-field fence.

The Rosemont team wandered around stunned. All eyes searched the horizon for the blast, but it was far gone.

Williams slowly trotted around the bases and defiantly challenged the Rosemont players with his sneer.

Coach La Russo called a time-out. He ran out of the dugout to the mound and signaled his players to gather around him.

"Listen up, guys. Forget that home run."

His words didn't seem to make an impact. He shouted at them, "Come on. We didn't come this far for nothing. What's the score?"

Glen came to attention first. "Two to one, Coach."

La Russo looked around at all his players. "So how many runs are we down?"

"One!" David started to get pumped up again. "One lousy run, Coach. That's all we need."

The other players started to loosen up. "Yeah. No problem."

"Okay then, let's—"

"*Do it!*" the team shouted.

Charged up again, the players slapped the pitcher on the butt, hustled back into position, and hollered encouragement.

Coach La Russo trotted back to the dugout, breathing a sigh of relief. He sat next to Roberto on the bench and said, "We've still got a chance. We just can't get down on ourselves."

"Don't worry, Coach. No quitters on this team. You'll see!"

Brian retired the next batter, and the entire Rosemont team seemed relieved. Going to the top of the sixth, it was only 2–1 against them.

Glen jumped down into the dugout and screamed, "Let's go, guys! We need some runs!"

"We can do it!" Roberto yelled. "C'mon, Ryan. Get us started."

Ryan Davis led off the inning for the Rockets. He waited patiently for a good pitch, and on a two-ball-and-two-strike count, laced a single to center. The dugout shouted out its encouragement.

Glen was next up. Looking down at the third-base coach, he picked up the sign for a hit-and-run. As soon as the pitcher made his move, the runner on first took off. The second baseman moved over to cover the bag for the throw to second. The pitch was a little outside, so Glen chopped down on the ball and bounced a single into right field through the hole left by the second baseman. Ryan raced to third. The play had worked perfectly.

"Attaway, Rockets. We're on our way!" La Russo cheered.

But on a three-and-two pitch, Jeff Brown took a third strike, and the next batter bounced back to the pitcher. In a split-second decision, the Central pitcher decided to go for the double play. He threw out Glen at second, and the second baseman whirled and drilled the ball to first.

"Safe," bellowed the umpire, and the tying run crossed the plate.

All the Rosemont players met Ryan at the plate and slapped high-fives. "All right, we got 'em . . . we got 'em. Way to go, Rye!"

The excitement wasn't even dampened when the next batter ended the inning, flying out to left field. Rosemont knew they were back in the ball game.

The score remained 2–2 entering the bottom of the eighth. Central Valley started the inning with a single. When the next batter singled, Coach La Russo sent Matthew Jackson out to the bullpen to start loosening up. Brian was getting tired.

"C'mon, Brian! You can do it. Hum it in there! Hum it in there!" the infield chanted.

On a three-and-two count, Brian threw a pitch into the dirt and walked the Central batter. The bases were loaded. Stepping up from the on-deck circle was Central Valley's first baseman . . . Jason Williams.

Walking out to the mound, Coach La Russo signaled to the bullpen. He took the ball from Brian's glove. "You pitched a great game, Holmes."

"C'mon, Coach. I can still do it. I don't want to go out!"

"You're getting tired. Besides, I want a right-hander throwing to Williams."

When Jackson reached the mound, La Russo handed him the ball and walked off the field with Brian Holmes. They went to the dugout to wait and watch.

Williams dug in at the plate and stared at Jackson.

Jackson looked down from the mound and shook his head. "I can't believe how big that guy is!" he thought to himself.

Sensing what was going through the pitcher's mind, Roberto yelled over to him, "He's got a big strike zone, Jackson. Make him work. Make him work!"

Plucking up his courage, Matthew threw a pitch that just missed the outside corner of the plate.

"Ball!" barked out the umpire.

"That's the way. Nibble the corners. You can do it!" Glen tried to bolster his pitcher's confidence.

Matthew's next pitch got away from him. It started out right down the middle of the plate.

Cringing, he knew disaster was about to strike.

Jason Williams coiled his body and unleashed a terrifying cut. The ball jumped off his bat as if it were jet propelled. Matthew couldn't even turn and watch.

Glen took two running steps and leaped. He thrust his body through the air as high and as far as it could go. Somehow, the web of his glove caught enough of the ball that it knocked it from its terrifying trajectory. The ball hung in the air a few seconds. Glen crashed to the ground and rolled over, just in time to see the ball dropping toward the ground. Scrambling on his hands and knees, he made one more desperate lunge and caught the ball as it was about to hit the ground.

Rolling on his side, Glen flipped the ball to the first baseman to double the runner off. The other Central base runners scrambled back to their bags safely.

For a moment, the crowd and players were speechless. The unbelievable play had everyone in a state of shock. Finally, the Rosemont bench screamed with joy.

"Outta sight!" "Fantastic, Mitch!" "Way to go, Scrapper!"

All Roberto could say, over and over again was, "*Unbelievable!*"

The play cut the heart out of the Central Valley team. Matthew struck out the next batter, and the Rosemont team swarmed into the dugout, fired up to a frenzy.

Screaming and yelling in the dugout reached a fever pitch, and when Rosemont's lead-off batter smashed a double, the roof almost came off.

Another hit, and then a walk, loaded the bases.

David Green strode to the plate with a purpose. Every player on the Rockets stood on the edge of the dugout steps.

They knew.

Central's pitcher had no place to hide. The first pitch he threw was a good one. David saw it, but knew it wasn't good enough. He jumped on it and sent a high, towering blast toward center field. It was the kind of shot that earned him his nickname . . . Downtown.

The center fielder made two steps toward the fence, and then just stood and watched.

All the Rocket players came charging out of the dugout, forming a line at home plate. One runner came home, the second runner crossed the plate, the third trotted in, and then came David. Savoring the moment, he'd gone into his best home-run trot. He finished with a resounding jump onto the plate, punctuating the end of Central Valley's reign as state champion.

Rosemont batted around in the top of the ninth and scored a total of seven runs. They then quickly retired Central in the bottom of the inning. The final score was 9–2.

After the last out, the players raced to celebrate out by the mound. A mob scene completely engulfed Glen, David, and Coach La Russo.

Running back into the locker room, the Rosemont team dashed through the showers, changed, and headed for the bus. Everybody was anxious to get back home and share the great news.

When they walked out the door of the locker room into the evening air, Glen pointed up to the poster of the Rocket mascot hanging in effigy. "Green . . . boost me up."

David lifted Glen up with a handhold, and Scrapper yanked the poster down.

"I told you guys we'd see who came out of this game alive!" he said as he crumpled up the brightly colored painting.

# SIX

"See you guys later," David shouted to his teammates as they left the Rosemont High parking lot. "Great ball game." The night was still too warm for a coat, so he threw his green-and-white letterman jacket over his shoulder and walked home.

David entered his family's white stucco house quietly, trying not to awaken anyone. His mother looked up from her ironing, neatly set up in the living room in front of the television, and smiled. Crossing both fingers, she asked, "Well? How'd it go?"

With a double thumbs-up signal, David beamed. "We did it, Mom! We clobbered 'em nine-two!"

"Oh, David, I'm so happy for you." She hugged

her son and kissed his forehead. "How'd *you* do? Tell me all about it!"

David flopped down on the well-worn sofa. "Mom, you should have seen it. Glen made this diving catch of a line drive with the bases loaded. It was the most spectacular catch I've ever seen. We were down two-one and it saved our lives."

"That's wonderful."

"It was two-two when we came up in the top of the ninth. . . .We loaded the bases and I . . ." pausing for effect, he then continued, "cleared 'em."

"A grand slam?"

"Right, Mom!" David beamed. Putting on a phony accent he drawled, "Aw shucks, Ma . . . it was nothing!"

Hugging her son, Carol Green fought back tears of pride. Her husband had taken off shortly after their seventh child was born, leaving her to fend for herself. David, at a very early age, had become the man of the house. Holding down part-time jobs after school, he worked hard to help his mother keep the family together.

"I'm so proud of you, honey!"

David could hear the emotion choking his mother's words. "C'mon Mom, let's celebrate. I'll get the ice cream outta the freezer."

As he walked toward the kitchen, he turned back to her. "Is anyone else still awake?"

A frown crossed her face. "Just Laurie."

David knew immediately what that meant. "Still not home, huh!" Glancing at his watch he saw it was ten-thirty. His fifteen-year-old sister was out late again.

"I don't know what to do with that girl. I've completely lost control of her."

"It's not your fault, Mom. Laurie's just kinda screwed up right now. I used to . . ."

"David, you never defied me like she does. I can't even speak to her without us fighting."

David leaned against the doorjamb between the kitchen and living room. His head slumped down into his chest. "I don't know what to do, either."

The sharp ring of the telephone interrupted them. David stepped toward the kitchen wall phone. "I'll get it."

Hoping it was his sister, he answered with a questioning voice. "Hello?"

David was surprised by the voice on the other end.

"Hello, David. I'm sorry to call so late, but I've had an emergency."

A lump formed in David's throat. His boss from work had never called him like this before. "What's up, Mr. Phifer?"

The owner of the neighborhood hardware store was upset. "Frank's wife just called. He's had an emergency appendectomy and won't be able to work this weekend. Larry's still out on vacation somewhere and I'm going to be at the trade convention this weekend. I'm afraid you're going to have to come in and give us a hand."

David cleared his throat. "Well . . . that'll be fine Sunday, but I can't work on Saturday. I've got a ball game."

"David, I need you on Saturday for the sale. That's going to be our busiest day."

"Yeah, but Mr. Phifer, Saturday's the state champion—"

His boss cut him off. "David, I don't give a damn about any game or whatever. I need you to work."

David heard the anger in his boss's voice and felt his own heart pounding. "You'll have to ask someone else for Saturday. . . ."

The voice on the other end was now very loud, almost screaming. "You don't understand, David. I'm not asking you to work this Saturday. I'm telling you to work. Can I make it any clearer? If I have to find someone else, it'll be on a permanent basis. Get it?"

With his back against the wall, David made a snap decision. "I've got it, all right! I quit!"

Dropping the phone back down in its cradle, David wandered over to the sink and leaned against the counter. His head was swimming. *Damn . . . I shouldn't have done that,* he said to himself. *Now what am I gonna do? We need that money.*

From the living room, his mother called out, "David?"

He rubbed his forehead. *What am I going to*

*tell Mom? She doesn't need this.* He went to the freezer and pulled out the vanilla ice cream.

Walking into the brightly lit kitchen she came up behind her son and asked, "Who was it on the phone? Laurie?"

The worry in her voice made David feel even worse. He knew he couldn't upset her now. "No, Mom. Just one of the guys on the team."

Disappointed, Carol Green shuffled over to the kitchen table and sat down.

David watched her for a second and then went to her side. Resting a hand on her shoulder, he said, "Two scoops, Mom?"

Placing her own hand on his, she smiled, "Two scoops, David. I think we need two scoops."

David rolled out of bed Friday morning and looked out his window. The sky was overcast but the temperature was warm.

Shaking the cobwebs from his mind, he thought to himself, *I'll bet it's going to be a hot summer. We're going to sell a ton of fans and air-conditioners.*

David caught himself in midsentence. Remembering the conversation of the night before he told himself, *Shoot, that's right, I don't have to worry about that. I don't work at Phifer's anymore.*

After showering and dressing, David popped his head into Laurie's bedroom. She was still asleep. He crossed the light-blue-and-gold-accented room and sat on the edge of her bed. He shook her once gently.

"Laurie . . . wake up."

With great difficulty, one of Laurie's green eyes started to crack open.

"Hey . . . time to get a move on," he shook her again, harder.

"Leave me alone . . . I'm skipping," she groaned.

"No, you're not." He yanked her pillow out from under her head.

"Uhhh! Don't do that to me."

"Then get up . . . now."

David's patience was lost, and Laurie knew it by the tone of his voice. She figured it was going to be lecture time.

"Okay, big brother. I'm up, I'm up." Pushing herself up with one elbow, she brushed her brown, shoulder-length hair from her forehead and focused directly on him. "What's with you?"

"You are . . . and Mom."

"So?"

"You tell me."

"There's nothing to tell," she sighed.

Crawling out of the opposite side of the bed, Laurie grabbed some clothes and headed for the bathroom. "Forget it, David. It's none of your business."

"Bull! This is *our* family." The emotion choking his voice caught her off guard.

"Yeah, I know. Just because you're older and work and—"

"I had to quit my job last night."

Laurie was surprised. "Why?"

"It doesn't matter. But Mom doesn't know yet. I couldn't tell her—especially last night. She was so bummed out about you."

Laurie sat silently.

"Look, Laurie. I'm a senior . . . I'm going to graduate soon. Mom's going to need your help around here more than ever. You two have to work through your hang-ups."

Shaking her head, Laurie groaned, "Fat chance."

David jumped to his feet and walked to the door. Pausing for a second, he stared at her. "Think about it!" he yelled and slammed the door shut.

"You're not my father!" she yelled. Throwing her clothes at the closed door, Laurie sank to her knees and cried.

Still excited about the previous day's game with Central Valley, Glen and Roberto barely made it through the Friday school day, anxiously awaiting baseball practice.

When the final bell rang, they stuffed their books into their lockers, changed into their practice gear, and sprinted off toward the field. David was already there.

"Hey, where've you been today?" Glen threw a ball at David.

Snapping it out of the air with one hand, David shrugged. "Just hanging around, like usual."

Roberto put on his glove and joined in the three-way game of catch. "You weren't at lunch."

David was evasive and angry. "I needed to get some school stuff done, so I went to the library to catch up. No big deal, guys. Just forget it."

"Sorrreee," said Glen. "Mr. Sensitive . . . we just wanted to know if you were okay."

Nodding his head, David calmed down. "Yeah. Really, guys, I'm okay."

Roberto clasped his hand around David's neck. "If you want to talk, don't forget that we're here. That's all."

"Thanks. I'll be fine."

As the rest of the team arrived at the practice field, they rolled around the lush green grass, stretching and loosening up. As captain of the team, David jumped to his feet and called all of his teammates together.

"Okay, guys, let's do our calisthenics before the coach gets out here." David moved backward and everyone fell into place on the field, spread an arm's length apart.

Just as the sweat was starting to form on everyone from the vigorous workout, Coach La Russo walked onto the diamond. "Looking good, guys." He playfully punched Bobby Judson in the stomach.

La Russo dropped a bag of equipment on the ground and said, "Ramirez, Mitchell, and Green . . . I want to see you in my office for a minute. The rest of you guys start running the drills. I'll be right back."

Roberto, Glen, and David gave each other questioning looks. They fell in line behind their coach and nervously walked back toward the old, red brick gymnasium.

As they walked across the field, Glen whispered to his friends, "What's happening?"

Two shrugs were his response.

They were momentarily blinded as they entered the dark building from the bright sunshine. Their spikes clanked against the white linoleum floor of the hallway. When they rounded the corner and saw Coach La Russo's office, they could see two men dressed in suits standing next to his desk.

All three boys gulped as they walked into the cramped quarters.

"Gentlemen, this is Roberto Ramirez, David Green, and Glen Mitchell. . . ." Pointing to each one as he spoke, La Russo completed the introductions. "Boys, I'd like you to meet a couple of the scouts who have been with us the past few games. From the Los Angeles Dodgers, this is Roy Palumbis, and this is Walt Charles from the Red Sox."

A tangled web of arms stretched across the room as handshakes were made.

Coach La Russo sat down at his old, gray metal desk. "Boys, I've known these two men for twenty years or so, and I've asked them in to talk to you."

Walt Charles spoke first. "Guys, the first thing I want to say is congratulations on a terrific season."

"So far!" said Glen.

Charles corrected himself immediately. "That's right. There's still one more big game to go. That's one of the reasons Coach La Russo asked us all to talk to you today. There's an awful lot of great baseball talent in Illinois, and especially in these state play-off games. The cream of the crop tends to rise in these pressure situations. That's why all of us scouts like to attend these play-off games."

Roy Palumbis broke in. "Walt's right. I'm sure it's no surprise to you boys that you've attracted a lot of attention; college recruiters, reporters, and scouts like us. We all feel that you have a future in baseball. Whether that's on the collegiate level or maybe even the professional level, no one knows yet. Our job is strictly to try and help our clubs evaluate that potential."

The three boys looked at each other. It was obvious they didn't know what to think.

Coach La Russo turned to his star players. "That's why I asked them to come in and talk to you. They weren't going to approach you until after the season was over, but I thought it would be better if we got the introductions out of the way so you guys could all just relax."

David and Roberto nodded. Glen said, "No problem."

Coach La Russo dismissed his three stars. "Go ahead and get back out to practice, guys, I'll be right there."

As they turned to leave, Roy Palumbis said, "Good luck in your next game."

Glen, David, and Roberto all managed the same reply. "Thanks."

As they drifted back down the hallway and out onto the ball field, the boys sorted through their thoughts privately. Finally Glen broke their silence. "Pretty interesting; huh, guys?"

Roberto shook his head. "I can't believe it."

Glen pushed his baseball hat back on his head. "The only thing that really matters right now is how we do tomorrow against East High. If we don't win that one . . ."

Roberto cut him off. "Don't even say it. It'll jinx it."

"Hey, what's our captain say about it all?"

David was staring off into the sky, avoiding eye contact with his friends. His mind was on a different wavelength than theirs. His problems at home and work were crashing down on him.

Glen nudged his friend. "Earth to Green, earth to Green. We're talking big stuff here."

# SEVEN

The afternoon of the big game arrived unseasonably hot and humid. It was the kind of day that reminded Roberto of his childhood in the Dominican Republic. Thinking back on those days, it seemed like an eternity to him since he'd left his homeland.

He paced the small patch of grass in his front yard and thought about the battle for the Illinois State championship. Rosemont's assistant coaches had given Roberto a detailed scouting report on East High the day before at practice. He went over it and over it all night.

Standing out by the front sidewalk, Roberto went into his motion and practiced pitching to each batter in his mind—a drill he liked to perform before the really important games, if he could.

Roberto's dad walked outside to join him. He'd just finished the Saturday-morning paper and wanted to talk to Roberto before the big game.

"How's it going, son?"

"I think I'm ready, Dad."

Carlos rubbed his son's arm and shoulder. "Tell me. This team you're playing today; they couldn't be as tough as Central Valley, could they?"

"I don't know. The coaches think that they haven't got the talent that Central has, but they've got attitudes . . . real tough attitudes."

The two Ramirezes sat down on a step of the front porch. "What does that mean?" the elder asked.

Roberto pulled a blade of grass apart as he spoke. "Well, Glen knows some of the guys on East's team. He also knows a little about the neighborhood over there. He says they're all tough kids. Ya know . . . street tough."

Carlos looked puzzled. "Where is East High? I guess I don't know anything about them."

"Lower east side of Chicago . . . near the old downtown area. They've had a lot of problems in the school with gangs, that kinda thing."

Roberto's dad shook his head. He remembered his own days as a tough kid growing up in Santo Domingo. Gangs were a fact of life for many of his friends even back then. "Listen . . .

I wanted to talk to you about college for a minute."

Roberto protested. "Gee, Dad. It's not a good time for me. My mind's kinda on the game."

"I understand that. But this is your last game, and it's getting pretty late to decide on a good college. Baseball is important now, but it's your education that's going to make you a success in this world. You can't forget that."

Roberto nodded. He was trying to concentrate on his father's words but found his mind drifting. "I know, Dad."

"Well, then. Let's buckle down here in the next few days and get your future organized, okay?"

"Sure . . . no problem." Roberto was irritated, finding it more difficult to be patient. He started to wander toward the front gate. "I'll figure it out after the game."

Relieved, Carlos sighed, "Medical school has always been our dream for you. A good college will really help you prepare properly."

Finally, Roberto couldn't take it anymore. He had to get moving. "Look, Dad. I guess I'm going to head on over to school. The coach wants us to go over a few things and then take the bus together to the game."

Standing, Carlos clasped his son's elbow. "Okay. Play well, and good luck. We'll be there cheering for you."

"Thanks, Dad. I'll catch ya later."

As he started walking down the sidewalk, his

father called out to him, "Roberto, don't you need your bag?"

Slapping his forehead, Roberto ran back to the house. Bounding up the stairs two at a time, he grabbed his equipment bag out of his bedroom and threw on his baseball hat. As soon as his hat was on, it seemed to change him. He stopped when he walked past the hall mirror and glanced at his reflection.

Tilting the hat back over his wavy black hair, he smiled and thought to himself, *Well, Magic Man. This is it . . . the big one . . . for all the marbles . . . do or die . . . make or break . . .* the championship game! *Are you ready?*

He pulled his cap back down to shade his eyes. Putting on his most ferocious stare, he snarled back at his reflection, "I was born ready!" He ran out of the house and down the street toward school.


Glen and David punched the door of the school gymnasium open and strutted toward the locker room. Glen's gray Nike bag was slung over his shoulder, and his baseball glove was already on his left hand. He pounded his fist into the mitt over and over again as he walked.

David leaned over and rammed his shoulder into Glen's. "Hey, you're going to wear yourself out, knothead. Slow down, will ya?"

"Stop worrying. Nothing's gonna slow me down today. I guarantee ya that."

Their tennis shoes squeaked as they shuffled down the hall.

Six or seven players were already in the locker room when David and Glen entered.

David immediately threw his bag to the ground and hoisted one of the big thirty-eight–ounce bats propped up against the wall. His vicious cut with the bat ended when it crashed against one of the towel baskets. The impact crushed in one side of the metal-and-canvas cart.

A chorus of insults filled the air.

"Nice shot, Green." "Way to go, ya big dummy." "I hope you can hit that well during the game."

Glen shook his head and laughed. "I can't believe you did that. And you were worried about *me!*"

David looked around sheepishly for the coach. Not finding him, he whispered, "We'll just keep this our little secret . . . right, guys?"

Boos echoed through the room. They stopped when the players noticed Coach La Russo enter the area. Apprehension played on each player's face.

"What the heck's going on in here?" he asked. "What're you guys booing about?"

Glen let his friend dangle just long enough to feel miserable. Then he said, "Nothing, Coach. I just said that this was probably going to be a tough game today. Everyone started jeering like they think we're going to kill 'em, I guess."

La Russo sensed there was more, but chose to ignore it. "Well, listen up, you guys. This *is* going to be a tough game. That's why I called everyone in early; so we could go over a few things. As soon as everyone gets here, let's get together in the gym. Understood?"

"Yes, sir!" rang out from the players. The seriousness in his voice put everyone on edge.

While Coach La Russo walked out one door toward his office, Roberto entered the other and approached his teammates. "Hey, what's happening?"

His teammates came and gave Roberto a hand slap or forearm smash. Glen sat down beside him on one of the wooden benches.

He twisted Roberto's cap bill around so it faced backward. "You ready to do it?"

Roberto smiled. "You know it."

Glen smacked him on the back. "All right, that's all I needed to hear!"

Pulling on his white baseball pants, Roberto hopped around on one foot. He lost his balance and crashed over into one of the metal lockers. A hushed silence stilled the air.

David ran over to his side. "Magic?"

Roberto looked up from the ground, clutching his pitching arm with a pained and worried look on his face. David's heart jumped to his throat.

Roberto then broke into a broad grin "Gotcha!"

The collective sigh of relief from the players was short-lived as towels, gloves, and hats were hurled at their star pitcher.

The underlying tension that had filled the locker room was broken for good. Laughter and the normal pre-game baseball chatter now drowned out the previous silence.

David, Glen, and Roberto finished putting on their uniforms, then put their tennis shoes back on. They wouldn't change into their cleats until they arrived at Civic Stadium, the site of the final game.

When everyone was ready, David led them into the gym. "C'mon, guys. Coach is waiting for us."

They circled around Coach La Russo when they entered the spacious arena and sat cross-legged on the hardwood floor. He waited for the shuffling around to stop.

"This has been one helluva season. I hope you all know how proud I am of you. There're a lot of cliché things to say here about how it doesn't matter who wins or loses this last game and all that, but I don't believe you guys need that."

He took a look around at his players. "I just want you to go out and play your best baseball. Use everything we've learned and worked on today. In games like this, physical skills are only part of it."

La Russo searched each player's eyes. "When

I went to Alabama to play football, I remember Bear Bryant had this plaque on the wall behind his desk. All of his players had to learn it by heart. It went like this: 'Life's races don't always go to the stronger or faster man. Sooner or later, the man who wins is the man who thinks he can.' I want you guys to remember that today . . . and the rest of your lives. Wherever you all wind up after you leave Rosemont, don't forget: learn, train, work hard . . . and be mentally tough."

Pausing to let his point sink in, he then raised his voice and yelled, "Now let's go win us a championship!"

The collective roar from the Rosemont team echoed throughout the gym.

The group leaving on the bus trip to Chicago Civic Stadium was loud and boisterous. As the stadium and game time approached, the mood became more subdued. When the Rockets finally arrived at the park, everyone was going through their own private preparations in silence.

Roberto looked out the bus window and saw the size of the stadium parking lot. He shook his head in disbelief, saying, "There must be a zillion people here. Look at all those cars!"

David overheard his comment and whispered back, "Two zillion."

The players marched in single file through a

throng of reporters and well-wishers gathered at the players' entrance. When they entered the cavernous underground world of the stadium, an attendant led them through the maze.

After they reached their designated locker room, Glen and David walked toward a patch of blue sky they saw through one of the gates. They stuck their heads out around the corner and looked out onto the field and the surrounding red seats.

"Geeez, this place is huge," David said.

Glen nodded in agreement. "It's gotta be as big as Wrigley. I betcha they could put over thirty thousand in here."

"Easy, man. Easy. I wonder how many will show up for this game. . . ."

The two boys turned and headed back to join the team. They finished changing into their cleats and waited for the word that it was their time to take practice.

When the Rosemont team started down the runway toward the field, a lump formed in Roberto's throat. "This is it, guys. I hope everyone's ready."

The team formed a circle and put their hands together. At just the right moment, they all yelled out, "Rockets!" and stormed out on the field.

The first thing David noticed was the red, white, and blue bunting hanging from the different balconies and walls around the field. The stands behind home plate and down both foul lines were filled with people. Even the bleachers in the outfield held a fair amount of fans.

Glen ran out and took note of the excellent condition of the field. The grass was a lush green, perfectly manicured and smoothly cut right down to where it meshed with the dirt infield. Examining the area around second base, Glen was amazed by the pebble-free soil.

"Perfect. Absolutely perfect," he mumbled to no one in particular.

When Roberto broke out into the afternoon sun, the first thing that struck his eyes were the colors of the East High Eagles.

*Sharp. Really sharp!* he thought to himself.

The Eagles wore royal blue hats with a silver, script E on the front. Their jerseys were a metallic, royal blue, and their pants were a silver that seemed to glisten in the bright daylight. He was dazzled by their professional appearance.

The Rockets were allowed thirty minutes for batting practice. East High had already taken theirs. David launched several blasts that brought some *ooh*s and *ahh*s from the crowd. Digging in at the plate, he felt right at home in the new ball park.

Rosemont then took infield practice and afterward, returned to their dugout. East High had the final warm-up period.

When both teams had finished their routines, the public-address announcer came on.

"Ladies and gentlemen. Welcome to the Illinois

State Baseball Championships . . . today featuring the Eagles from East High . . ."

A loud chorus of cheers went up from behind the Eagles dugout.

". . . against the Rosemont High Rockets!"

Another explosion of support came from behind their side of the field.

The announcer then proceeded to introduce all the players on each team. One by one, they ran out and stood on the foul lines extending from home plate. After all the players and coaches were called, the organist fired up his rendition of the national anthem, and the fans joined the players in standing at attention.

The players grew anxious when they were subjected to a ceremonial first pitch—this one thrown by the mayor of Chicago. It took several efforts before the cameramen got all the pictures they wanted.

But after all the pomp and circumstance was finally completed, the players ran back to their dugouts. The coaches went to home plate and exchanged lineup cards. And then, what everyone had been waiting for, the home-plate umpire screamed out at the top of his lungs, *"Play Ball!"*

# EIGHT

Rosemont High's baseball team dashed out on the sun-drenched field when they heard the umpire's call. Coach La Russo paced up and down the length of the dugout. His goal was for the Rockets to shut down the East High offense and immediately establish control of the game. With his ace on the mound, he was confident they could do it.

Roberto strolled out to the mound. Stuffing a huge wad of bubble gum in his cheek, he slowly worked it into place while he carefully rubbed up the baseball. He made a special effort to inhale through his nose and exhale gently through his mouth. It was all part of a pregame ritual he used to make sure he didn't rush his pitches.

After his nine warm-up tosses, Roberto stepped to the side of the mound as the catcher fired the ball out to second. From there it was whipped quickly around the infield, until the third baseman came in and flipped him the ball.

Rosemont's infielders started their incessant chatter, trying to fire up their own pitcher and distract the batter at the plate.

"Hum it in there, hum it in there . . ." "Hey, hey!" "Atta, baby, atta, baby, you can do it. . . . C'mon, Magic . . . you can do it." "Swing, batta, swing. Swing, batta, swing."

East High's lead-off batter dug a foothold for himself in the batter's box. A few quick practice swings and he cocked his "Black Magic" aluminum bat back, ready for the first pitch.

The crowd noise rose as fans yelled encouragement to the team or player they were rooting for. Roberto took a quick glance around the stands, searching for his family. The size of the crowd made it impossible to spot them.

Roberto stared down at his catcher. Picking up the sign from between the catcher's two orange kneepads, Roberto nodded and began his windup.

"Here we go now. Let's make it good," Roberto said to himself.

His fastball zipped across the inside corner of the plate. The batter never moved. The umpire bellowed, "*Striiiike* one!"

Roberto smiled to himself, partially in satisfaction, partially in relief.

His arm spun back and then whirled forward as his body rocked on the rubber. This time, a meek swing resulted in the second strike.

The batter stepped out of the box, looked to his coach in the dugout, and shrugged.

Roberto nodded with approval when he saw his catcher's signal. Having worked together for two years, Scott Brodie and Roberto were on the same wavelength. They both knew the curve ball was the right pitch.

The East High batter swung three feet in front of the slowly breaking curve ball and knew he'd been had.

"*Striiiike* three, you're outta there!" the umpire yelled.

The Rockets' infield raised the level of their chattering. "Wayda go, Magic, wayda go!"

Glen turned and gave a thumbs-up sign to David out in center field. Their tension was relieved by getting off to a good start.

Roberto worked carefully on the next East High batter. His scouting reports had warned him that Jeff Walters was a dangerous contact hitter. True to form, with two strikes and one ball on him, he managed to get a good piece of the pitch and drive it out toward center. But David had plenty of time to run under it and make the catch, for the second out.

When the third batter hit a routine three-hopper to Glen, who fired to first in plenty of time, the inning was over and the pregame jitters gone.

David made the long run in from center field and swung down into the dugout. "Good job. Magic. Good job. Wayda fire."

Roberto stood at one end of the dugout and listened to the encouragement and support of his teammates. He'd never seen his teammates so fired up.

Coach La Russo worked his way down the dugout and rubbed Roberto's shoulder. "Nice work, Ramirez. Keep the ball down on these guys, all right?"

"I'll try, Coach." Roberto could sense the anxiety in his coach's words.

Glen stood next to David and watched the East High team go through their warm-ups. Their movements were full of flash and showmanship. Glen was starting to get upset.

"Hey, DT. Have you been watching these clowns out there?"

David brought his gaze down from the far reaches of the stadium and focused on the Eagles. "I don't see anything so special."

"They've got one wicked attitude, man. They're starting to tick me off!"

David reached down and flipped a batting helmet up toward his friend. "Here. Put this on and worry about hitting. Not what those guys look like."

"Hey . . . I'm not kidding ya. They're a bunch of cocky wise guys. . . . They think they're gonna beat us."

"And they will if you don't get your head in

the game. Now, c'mon. Forget it." David was getting irritated with his friend.

As the first Rocket batter hit a single bouncer to the shortstop and made the first out, Roberto shuffled over and joined David and Glen. "What's up with you guys?" he asked. "What're you arguing about?"

"We're not arguing," David said. "Glen here thinks the East High team isn't showing us proper respect, that's all."

Roberto nodded. "I thought they were kinda showing off myself during pregame. I didn't think anyone else noticed."

"I noticed, all right," said Glen. "Especially that smart-alec pitcher of theirs, Robinson. I'm gonna show him a thing or two."

"He one of the guys you know?"

"Yeah. I went to a baseball camp last summer, and he and I had a run-in."

"What happened?" Roberto asked.

Glen didn't answer. Instead, he whacked down hard on the top of his batting helmet and went to the on-deck circle, waiting for his turn at bat.

The next Rosemont batter hit a high pop fly. East High's catcher circled around in front of the plate, threw his mask far to the side, and made the grab. Two were out.

Glen couldn't take his eyes off East's pitcher as he approached the plate. He took his spot in the box and dug in with his right foot. The white chalk line marking the batter's box was already completely obliterated.

Cocking his bat back, Glen sneered out at the mound. He muttered under his breath, "Try and get it past me, meathead."

East's pitcher, Johnny Robinson, laughed as he looked down at Glen. "How ya doing, Mitchell? Long time, no see."

Glen dug in deeper and let his bat point directly at the pitcher at the end of his practice swing.

Robinson went into his windup and unleashed his pitch. The fastball came rising in, hard and fast, and before he knew it, Glen had to dive down to avoid the beanball.

The ball just missed the brim of his green batting helmet. Glen jumped up and took two steps toward the mound, but the voices of his friends and coach stopped him.

"C'mon, Glen. Stay in the game."

Brushing the dirt from his green jersey, Scrapper stepped back toward the plate. He fanned his red hair back and forth quickly to knock the dust out before putting on his helmet again.

When he stepped into the box again, Glen looked out and saw the smile on the pitcher's face. "You're gonna pay for that, Robinson!" he yelled out.

The East High pitcher continued to grin. "Send me a bill, Mitchell . . . I'll deduct it from what ya owe me!"

"I don't owe you squat, chump—" Glen was cut off in mid-insult.

"Let's play ball here and stop the word games, gentlemen, or I'll ask you to leave the ball game. Do I make myself understood?" The home-plate umpire's words left nothing to their imagination.

Glen silently stepped up to bat.

The East High hurler fired two fastballs by Glen for two quick strikes. His swing was just a little late to make contact. Then Robinson wound up and fired a sweet curve ball that deftly cut across the outside corner of the plate. Glen never got his bat off his shoulder when he winced as the umpire called the third strike.

Ramming his bat back into the rack, Glen watched as Robinson swaggered off the mound. Glen was still grumbling when he grabbed his glove and raced out on the field.

Coach La Russo knew that his team didn't feel good about being retired so quickly. "C'mon, you Rockets," he yelled. "Let's fire up out there. Look alive, look alive."

Roberto got into a groove and started throwing everything where he wanted. He retired the side with only eight pitches. He felt strong and allowed himself a brief smile as he walked toward the dugout.

"All right, let's see what this guy's got," David yelled as he ground his hands into the end of his bat. He walked to the plate with stony-eyed determination.

Robinson glared right at him, mocking the seriousness in David's eyes. Twisting the bat tighter in his grip, David wanted to launch a shot right back up the middle.

"Hey, Mr. Home Run Champ. Here's one for you!" Robinson yelled as he went into his windup. The pitch started directly for David's head.

DT leaned back in the box and watched sheepishly as the ball broke down and away from him for a called first strike.

Robinson gripped the ball in his left hand and held it hidden in his glove. He fired the second pitch right at David's knee with a sweeping sidearm motion. It, too, came in over the plate and the umpire called, "Strike two!"

Angry with himself, David was so rattled he swung at the third pitch as it bounced into the ground in front of home plate. The East High catcher had to field it and throw to first on the dropped third strike. David tried to hustle to the bag, but the ball beat him there. All he could do was curse under his breath as he walked back to the dugout. Two more batters had similar results, and Rosemont was back in the field.

Glen walked to the mound with his friend Roberto. "Hold 'em down, guy. We'll get you some runs eventually."

Roberto studied Glen carefully. "How tough is Robinson? Is there something you're not telling?"

# NINE

Roberto pitched magnificently. His fastball was blazing and his curve ball danced all over the place. Equally impressive, Robinson matched him pitch for pitch. For the next two innings of the title game, neither team could get a man on base.

As he walked off the mound after the top of the fifth, Roberto glanced up at the scoreboard and saw the string of zeroes. No runs, no hits, no errors—for either team.

David found his bat and headed to the plate to lead off the bottom of the fifth. Robinson was in complete command of his pitches and worked with a cocky smile on his face. David dug in and waited. *I'd love to wipe the grin off that guy's face,* he thought.

The first pitch came in low and on the inside corner. David wheeled around, caught it with his vicious swing, and sent a long drive out toward right field. The wicked line shot was still rising when it cleared the outfield fence. But it had twisted foul, missing the foul pole by inches, resulting only in a long first strike.

"Shoot!" David screamed as he kicked at the dirt. "Six lousy inches, that's all, just six lousy inches!"

Roberto bellowed out from the dugout, "You can do it, DT. Hang in there!"

For the first time in the game, the Eagle's pitcher looked concerned. Knowing he'd made a good pitch and still seeing it hit out of the park, he decided to be a little more careful with David. He worked the count carefully to three and two, and then threw a sharp-breaking curve ball toward the inside corner.

David froze for an instant, and then decided to take the pitch. He felt instant relief when he heard the call, "Ball four. Take your base."

He was the first base runner of the game.

The Rosemont bench erupted in cheers. "Atta way, DT. Make him work, make him work. That's a start . . . now we're going."

David danced off first, trying to distract the East High pitcher. But Robinson was cool. He tugged at his jersey and adjusted his hat while he stood on the rubber. He went into his stretch. He paused for what seemed an eternity before delivering his pitch to the plate. The Rosemont team screamed from the dugout.

But their cheers were short-lived. The batter bounced into a routine double play. The fire was out. When Craig Whitcomb struck out to end the inning, the Rockets were depressed and disheartened.

Coach La Russo tried his best to get his team motivated. Clapping his hands, he yelled out from the dugout, "C'mon, you guys. You can do it. Keep your heads in the game. This is what we've been working for all year. Don't forget who and what you are!"

After finishing his warm-up tosses, Roberto turned around to check out his teammates. He saw them kicking at the dirt, arms folded, heads down, unusually quiet. Spirit was low.

Fighting back his own growing tension, Roberto continued to force the Eagles into hitting ground balls—and even that didn't happen very often. In the seventh inning he struck out the side. Through those seven innings he'd fanned fifteen batters.

Going into the top of the eighth inning, both pitchers still had no-hitters. Roberto was throwing a perfect game.

With one out in the eighth, East High's pitcher, Johnny Robinson, came to the plate.

The catcher walked up to the mound. "Hey, Magic. I think you'd better work this guy carefully. He's a pretty good sticker."

Roberto nodded. "Yeah, he's a pretty decent

hitter . . . especially when the game's on the line."

"Right. Keep it outside and down, so if he does make contact he can't hurt us with a long ball."

"Gotcha." Roberto gave the "okay" sign to his friend.

Jumping out in front of the hitter with two quick strikes, Roberto tried to get him to swing at a couple of bad pitches. Robinson would have nothing to do with them and waited patiently in the box for a good pitch.

The count finally worked up to three balls and two strikes. Roberto hit the outside corner of the plate, but Robinson managed to get a piece of it and foul it off.

After four foul balls, Roberto misfired. His perfect game was over. Johnny Robinson trotted down to first base with a walk . . . the first base runner of the game for the Eagles.

Robinson couldn't resist the temptation as he eased off the bag. "Hey, Ramirez . . . ya losing it?"

Ignoring him, Roberto reached for the rosin bag and slowly rubbed up the ball. But Glen couldn't let the comment go.

"We're not losing anything, Robinson."

The East High star stared at him with mock terror in his eyes. "The nightmare's just beginning, Mitchell."

Glen took a step toward his antagonist. "In your dreams!"

Roberto screamed out at his teammate. "Hey, Scraps . . . cool it! Get back in the game."

Glen turned his back on Robinson and assumed his playing position at second. He led the infield banter, trying to charge up his teammates.

"Let's go, Rockets. Fire up, fire up. These guys ain't nothing. Hum it in there, Magic, hum it in there."

The rest of the team started to feel the adrenaline flow again. "You can do it, Magic. Strike him out, strike him out."

Roberto worked from the stretch to hold the runner close at first. He shook off the sign from Brodie, his catcher. He wanted to throw a fastball. When they connected on the sign, Roberto wound up and delivered.

The East High batter hit a high chopper toward shortstop. John Matthews gloved it and made the toss to second. Scrapper was there, gliding across the bag. He caught it and was about to relay to first for the double play.

Although Glen was already past the bag, Robinson had swung wide of the base path and came sliding in with his cleats up. As he started to flip through the air, Glen managed to fling the ball to first, making it just in time to catch the runner streaking toward first for the double play.

Robinson's cleats caught Glen right above the ankle. They tore through the heavy material of his pant leg and sock and ripped into the exposed skin. Unable to get up, he watched the blood start to flow.

The Rosemont bench rose and started a charge onto the field. It was all Coach La Russo could do to prevent a brawl.

"Stop right there, you guys. Nobody leaves the bench," he screamed at the top of his lungs. "I'll handle this!"

At a speed that defied his size, La Russo was at Glen's side in an instant. "How bad, Mitchell?"

Glen peered up through eyes squinched with pain. He saw the entire Rosemont team surrounding him. "Did we get the double play?"

"Yeah," La Russo said, nodding.

"Then"—trying to move his leg out from under him, Glen grunted, "it's not too bad."

The trainer, Ken Bush, was there spraying the gash with disinfectant and wrapping it with gauze and tape. "We'll clean it out when we get to the hospital," he told Coach La Russo.

Glen started to stand up on his good leg. "That'll have to wait, then. I ain't going anywhere until we win this game!"

David grabbed one arm and Roberto the other. Together they helped their teammate and friend off the field. When they reached the dugout and plopped him down on the bench, they heard Coach La Russo yelling.

"Okay, men. Gather 'round." His face was puffed out and his forehead was glowing red with anger. "To my way of thinking, that was a cheap shot. That's not the way the game was meant to be played. It wasn't the first one in this game. . . ."

He looked out across the field toward Johnny Robinson, warming up on the mound. "And the way things are going, it probably won't be the last. But we didn't work as hard as we have all year for nothing. We've made a lot of sacrifices and fought hard—hard and clean—to get here. It's not going to end like this."

He looked down at Glen. "We're going to keep giving it all we've got. And we're going to win. We're going to show the East High Eagles that you don't intimidate the Rockets. You don't intimidate this team in any way, shape, or form."

His voice rose in emotion and decibel level with each sentence. "Because we have the stuff that champions are made of, Glen turned that double play. Roberto's pitching a no-hitter, and *we will not be denied!*"

The Rockets exploded in a raucous cheer. Charged to a fever pitch, the Rosemont team started smashing gloves, bats, hats, and balls against the dugout wall and screaming out their conviction.

The East High team stood in the field and stared into the Rosemont dugout.

Johnny Robinson pounded the ball into his glove and wiped his brow with his forearm. For the first time in the game, he looked nervous.

The first batter of the inning, Scott Brodie, watched Robinson throw four straight pitches outside. He trotted down to first with a base on balls. The noise from the Rocket dugout was deafening.

"Atta way, Scotter. Wayda go."

But again, the rally attempt was stalled when the next two batters were victims of Robinson's unhittable curve balls, and they struck out.

Tommy Noble, sent up to pinch-hit for Glen, grabbed two bats and swung them as he walked toward the plate. As Coach La Russo approached the umpire to announce the change, Glen jumped off the bench and hobbled out of the dugout.

"Coach . . . wait."

La Russo turned around to see his second baseman with a bat in his hand. He turned and went to Glen's side.

"You can't do it, Mitchell. You can't put any weight on that leg."

"C'mon, Coach. I didn't come this far to be benched. Besides, I don't need to put any weight on it. It's my front foot, so I can just stay back, keep my weight on the right foot."

La Russo shook his head. "I can't let you do it, Mitchell."

"Coach, ya gotta. There's no reason to save me for tomorrow. There is no tomorrow. This is it."

Standing silently, La Russo tried to think of a way to ease his star out of the game.

Glen wouldn't let him. He stared up at his coach with pleading eyes. "I can hit this guy,

Coach. Believe me. Besides, he's gotta pay for this."

La Russo couldn't say no. He slapped him on the back. "Go do it, kid."

Glen gave the thumbs-up sign to the dugout. The team cheered wildly. David ran out with a batting helmet and stuffed it down on Glen's head.

"Don't do anything stupid up there, Scraps. I want ya to take care of yourself."

Glen smiled. "Don't worry, DT. I'm just gonna set the table. You got to clean it up."

Mitchell shuffled slowly up to the batter's box and tried to find a comfortable stance. He spread his stance apart, but the weight on his left leg made him wince. Glancing down, he saw the gauze bandage starting to turn crimson red.

Robinson checked the runner at first and then looked out at the scoreboard. It was the bottom of the eighth and still not a single hit for either team. He peered at the plate and got his sign, woundup, and pitched.

The ball came breaking inside and headed directly for Glen's front leg. Scrapper pushed off his back foot at the last possible instant and jumped into the air, just avoiding the pitch. The ball bounded past the catcher and Scott Brodie raced down to second.

Glen yelled out to the mound. "You're gonna have to throw harder than that if you wanna hit me, jackass!"

Robinson stomped around out on the mound.

Glen was getting under his skin. "No problem, sucker," he muttered, gritting his teeth.

Glen pounded the plate with his bat as Robinson started his delivery. The pitch was a blazing fastball out over the far corner of the plate. In the split second of time he had to analyze it, Glen decided on his best option. He shortened his stroke, leaned out over the plate a little, and slapped at the ball with his bat.

The fat part of the bat made solid contact, and the ball took off on a line. The first baseman took two steps toward the hole and jumped. The ball streaked just over the outstretched edge of his glove into right field.

Glen took off toward first and immediately realized he couldn't run. He created a hop-skip motion and slowly fought his way toward first. The ball wasn't hit very deep, and the right fielder grabbed it after a few bounces and came up firing. The ball and Glen reached first within an eyelash of each other. The umpire's hands spread out as he yelled, "Safe!"

Scott had to hold at third on the short single, but the entire Rosemont team stormed out on the field to cheer Glen. The score was still nothing to nothing, but he'd broken up the no-hitter.

Coach La Russo immediately signaled for a pinch runner and sent Tommy Noble in for Glen. David was the first by his side to congratulate him.

"Wayda go, Scraps. You're an amazing guy!"

"Hey, I told you I'd set the table. I did my part, you just do yours."

David nodded and smiled. "Piece of cake, Mitchell. Get the odometer out for this one. It's going for a ride."

Glen smiled.

David stood in at the plate and waited for the first pitch. Robinson stepped off the mound and worked some rosin into his glove. He took his sign from the catcher, reared back, and threw.

The pitch came in high and tight and sent David crashing to the ground. Coach La Russo was out of the dugout on his way to the mound when the first-base umpire stopped him.

The home-plate umpire stalked out to the mound. With his blue suit stretched tight over his six-foot frame, he was an imposing figure. "That's it, Robinson. I won't have any more of that throwing at the batters, or you're outta here. Understand?"

"It just slipped. I didn't—" Johnny's eyes were wide in faked amazement.

"I don't want to hear it. I see anything else come within three feet of a batter and I'm tossing you. End of subject. Period!" The umpire then turned and walked to the East High dugout. He repeated his warning to the Eagle's coach, and then resumed his position behind the plate.

The Rosemont players screamed from the bench like a lynch mob. It was everything La Russo could do to keep his players from storming the field. But the look in David Green's eyes calmed him down.

He'd seen the look before. He hadn't played and coached baseball for over thirty years without learning something. The look in David's eyes said it all.

"C'mon, Green. Let it happen," he yelled from his perch on the dugout steps.

The Rosemont players cried out, "Let's go, DT. You can take him. He's all yours now."

Knowing that David loved fastballs, Robinson waited for the catcher to signal a curve. When he got it, he nodded and started his windup. The pitch came in high and inside, just like the first pitch of the game to him. But this time, David stood in there. He waited for the pitch to break down over the plate, and then he took over.

His bat lashed out in a ferocious uppercut. The meat of the bat caught the pitch squarely. The ball took off on an awesome trajectory. There was nothing for anyone to do but watch.

The Rockets bench ran out of the dugout as soon as the ball was hit. David slammed his bat down into the ground and stood and watched. He slowly started to trot to first as the stands started to cheer. It had taken them a second to realize what was happening.

The ball cleared the third deck of Civic Stadium and disappeared over the street bordering the park. Scott Brodie came in and jumped on home plate. Tommy Noble trotted in over the plate. David Green circled the bases and headed for home. A double line of team-mates slapped high-fives with him as he came down the third-base line. He made a monster jump onto home plate to punctuate the dramatic homer. Rosemont was ahead, 3–0.

"DT, DT, DT," the chant rose from his teammates.

"Outta sight!" "Unbelievable!" "Wayda go!"

The cheers followed him to the dugout.

Coach La Russo greeted him at the steps of the dugout. He threw an arm around David's shoulders and hugged him. "You're all right, Green. Ya know that?"

David saw the huge grin on his coach's face. "Hey, Coach, I'm playing with the best."

After the mob scene subsided, David sat down next to Glen. "How's the leg, Scraps?"

"Don't feel a thing," he said with a smile. "Not now!"

Rosemont's next batter grounded out during the dugout celebration, to end the inning. It was up to Roberto to finish off the game.

Still excited from the dramatic three-run rally, Roberto tried to blaze his first four pitches by East's lead-off batter. Horribly overthrown, the pitches sailed high and he walked him.

Brodie went out to the mound to calm his pitcher down. "Hey, Magic, just settle down. You're trying too hard."

Roberto nodded. "Yeah, I know. I'm sorry."

As his catcher returned to the plate, Roberto

worked the ball with his hands and stared out at the huge scoreboard in center field.

He mumbled to himself, "C'mon . . . just over the plate. That's all it takes."

He worked from the stretch and took his sign. Watching the runner at first, he fired his next pitch low into the ground.

"Ball one," the umpire called.

"You can do it, Magic. Hum it in there. You can do it!"

Magic continued to struggle. He managed to get a strike over the plate but wound up walking the second batter, too. The tying run was now coming to the plate.

Coach La Russo ran up the dugout steps and out to the mound. He knew Roberto was in trouble.

"Hey, ace. Settle down. You don't have to do it all yourself."

"Sorry, Coach. I'm trying. . . ."

"I know . . . you're trying too hard. Take a deep breath and calm down."

Roberto weakly nodded his head.

La Russo walked back toward the plate with the catcher, Scott Brodie. "Tell me the truth, Brodie. How's his arm? His pitches still coming in strong?"

"He's still firing, Coach. There's plenty of zip there, I think he's just overthrowing a little."

"Signal me if you see a change, okay?"

La Russo turned toward the dugout. He yelled out to Roberto, "Take your time. You can do it."

Roberto took a look around the infield and wiped the sweat from his forehead. He searched the overflowing stands for his family. He thought he heard a solitary, pleading voice rise above the din: "C'mon Robbie, just three more outs."

He finally spotted his mother standing and waving her arms. A smile crept across his face. He tipped his hat toward her and relaxed. *Three more outs, huh? I guess I can handle that,* he thought to himself.

Turning his attention back to the batter, Roberto stared down for the sign from his catcher. He snapped off a brilliant curve ball and heard the umpire call out, "Strike one."

"That's more like it," he whispered to himself. "Two more just like it should do the trick."

Brodie's call for another curve ball was no surprise. He knew it would slow Roberto down and get him back in the groove.

The next pitch Roberto threw came streaking in toward the plate, and then dropped like it fell off a tabletop. The batter waved his bat at it in a hopeless attempt at contact. "Strike two," yelled the umpire.

For the third pitch, Roberto reared back and fired his fastball. East High's batter never had a chance. Caught flat-footed from the previous two curve balls, he stood and watched as the third strike blazed by him.

The Rosemont players screamed wildly.

"Two more, Magic, just two more."

"Wayda go, Magic Man."

The butterflies in Roberto's stomach started flying again. A million thoughts floated around in his mind. The pressure was bringing a lump to his throat.

*Geez. Two outs away from the state championship.* He fought to focus his thoughts. *Two outs away from a no-hitter!*

He stepped off the mound and rubbed the baseball tightly in his hands. He watched East High's cleanup hitter, Josh Reynolds, step into the box. He knew the job wasn't getting any easier.

Roberto toed the pitching rubber and checked the runners on first and second. Reynolds was East High's long-ball hitter. Roberto knew he'd be looking to tie up the game with one swing of the bat.

David restlessly roamed back and forth across the outfield. "Come on, Magic," he muttered. "Get it over with." The pressure was eating away at him.

The Eagles were standing on the top step of the dugout, screaming out their encouragement to Reynolds. The Rockets were nervously pacing around the field, pounding their gloves and yelling out their support for Roberto.

Glen felt absolutely nothing in his leg. All he could do was cup his hands and call out to his friend, "C'mon, Magic. You can do it . . . you can do it!"

The two coaches were dying a thousand

deaths. There was nothing they could do now to influence the outcome. It was all up to their players. Knowing that they had their stars out there to do the job was their only consolation. The game would be decided by their best.

Roberto started the stretch, paused, and then fired his pitch toward the plate.

Reynolds saw the fastball coming in on the inside corner and coiled his entire body. He unleashed the full fury of his swing at just the right moment and made solid contact. The ball flew off his bat like a fighter plane rocketing off an aircraft carrier.

Roberto sucked in his breath in a moment of sheer panic. He knew he'd made a mistake. His mind went blank as all his hopes, dreams, and fears collided in a rush to control his thoughts.

David took a step in the direction of the ball and then froze. It wasn't going to be his play.

The Rosemont first baseman, Ryan Messick, threw his glove up in front of his face. It was a matter of self-defense. The ball had rocketed down to first so fast, his only move was to protect himself. The ball smacked into his glove and fell to the ground.

Ryan scooped up the ball and hurled it to second. The shortstop floated across the bag, made the relay throw back to Ryan, and in a stunning turn of events, the game was over.

The game-ending double play happened so fast, it took a second before anyone realized what had happened. Glen was the first player off the Rocket's bench. He hopped, skipped, and jumped out to the mound and leaped into Roberto's arms.

David flew in from the outfield and high-fived Roberto, then grabbed his two friends up in a giant bear hug. The rest of the team came circling in and piling onto the group at the mound. In a matter of seconds, the entire team was buried in a huge pile of waving, screaming, deliriously happy kids.

"Champions!" "We did it . . . we won it all!"

The chant went up. "We are number one! We are *number one!*"

After watching the joyous celebration for a moment, the East High team silently filed off the field and into their dugout. Second in the state didn't sound too good to them at the time.

The Rosemont team continued their chant and were joined by their fans. Streaming out of the stands, students, families, and friends flooded the field and reveled in the thrilling victory.

As the uproar slowly subsided, Glen, David, and Roberto made their way off the field and sat down together in the dugout.

"Well, guys, we did it." David punched the air with his closed fist. "State champions . . . *numero uno.*"

Roberto laughed. "We're *numero uno*? Sounds strange."

"But true," said Glen. "Number one. Man, that

sounds good." Punching Roberto in the shoulder, he continued, "And, let's not forget Mr. No-hitter here. Nice time to look good out there. Magic Man."

"He's gonna have his pick of schools after this," David said. "There'll be no living with him anymore."

Roberto pushed his friends, seated on either side of him, away. "Get outta here. You guys are the ones who won the game. If we don't score, I could be out there all night and never win. Nobody remembers the pitcher yanked with a dead arm after eleven innings. They just remember who won the game."

David nodded his head. "We all did."

Glen reached down and fiddled with his bandage. The blood had stopped flowing, but the pain was back in full force. Roberto noticed his discomfort.

"C'mon, DT, we'd better get this guy somewhere to take care of that leg."

The two of them helped Glen to his feet. They each held one of his arms around their neck, trying to support him. As they walked out of the dugout, Glen stopped them and paused to look out at the huge stadium, the sun sinking below its rim. "You know, guys, this is it. We've worked hard for this moment; it doesn't seem right that it's going to end."

David softly agreed. "Yeah, I know what you mean."

# TEN

Rosemont High School's student body tingled with excitement. The school was packed with politicians, board members, dignitaries, and media people. It seemed everyone wanted to ride the wave of good feeling created by the Rockets baseball team. Everybody who was anybody showed up Monday morning for the ten-o'clock awards assembly.

Colorful banners and hand-painted posters hung everywhere, each illustrating some aspect of the 3–0 victory over East High for the state championship. Rosemont High had waited a long time to celebrate an important victory, and they weren't going to miss the chance.

Glen, David, and Roberto sat patiently through speech after speech. All they really wanted to do was get their hands on the huge, gold-engraved trophy. But before that hardware would be presented, there was lots of praise and thanks to be handed out.

Stifling a yawn, Glen leaned his head toward David. "I wish they'd cut this crap and get to the good stuff."

"You know it. I just hope the coach doesn't get carried away with all this, too." David glanced over to Coach La Russo. "Good news . . . no notes. I think he's just gonna wing it."

Glen chuckled. "At the rate this assembly's going, he won't have time to speak unless we skip lunch period."

Fidgeting in his seat, Roberto struggled inwardly. He couldn't decide whether he should share his news or not. Unable to control himself any longer, he nudged his buddies and leaned forward in his chair. "I got a call from the coach at University of Michigan. He said he was going to be here today and wanted to meet me," he whispered.

Glen and David's eyes widened in astonishment. Glen slapped him on the knee. "That's fabulous, Magic! Why didn't you tell us before?"

"I don't know. I guess I feel kinda weird about it."

"Weird? I don't believe it." David shook his head. "Well . . . did he say anything about a scholarship, or what?"

"We didn't talk that much. He just said he

wanted to come down and meet me and my family today and sit down with all of us. My mom's pretty thrilled about it."

Glen stared cross-eyed at him. "And your old man isn't?"

"Well, yeah . . . I guess. He's more concerned about pre-med programs and scholastic stuff."

David nodded. He started to question Roberto, but saw Coach La Russo out of the corner of his eye staring at them. He immediately clammed up.

Glen whispered out of the corner of his mouth, "We'll talk as soon as we get out of here." He twisted his head around, looking in all directions. "Now . . . where's that trophy?"

After Coach La Russo said a few words, the big moment arrived. "David, will you come up with me, please?" he asked.

As captain of the team, David and Coach La Russo were to accept the trophy. They stood nervously on the stage, looking around for what was to happen next.

The side doors of the gym opened and in walked Stan Grady, the Illinois State Athletic Association chairman, lugging the gigantic award. He made his way up to the microphone and spoke only three words. "To the *champions* . . ."

David and La Russo hoisted the symbol high in the air. They turned first toward the rest of the team behind them, and then to the students sitting out front. Bedlam broke out as the cheers echoed through the gym. Any further speeches were impossible.

One by one, the Rocket players came up and held the trophy above their heads. Roberto's eyes burned when he held the honored prize above him. He looked out over the whole gym and the cheering students, and realized that his high-school days were numbered, and this scene was one he didn't want to forget.

"That was really something, wasn't it?" David said to his two buddies as they stepped into the fresh air after the assembly broke up. The sun poked down through the clouds and seemed to focus directly on them.

Neither Glen nor Roberto answered, both lost in their own thoughts.

David tried again to get their attention. "I think school's gonna be a bore today. Whatta you guys think?"

"You know it," Glen mumbled. "I feel like cutting . . . how about it?"

The three boys looked at each other with mischievous grins.

Roberto shook his head. "I don't know when that guy from Michigan is going to show up, or where. I guess I'd better stick around. How great would it look if he finds out I'm skipping school?"

"Yeah. It's not worth the risk. You guys are

probably gonna wind up someplace great if you hang in there and finish off the year," David said.

Glen did a double take. "And you're not?"

David looked away. "I think I'm gonna stay here at Clairmont Community College so I can still work. I don't think my mom could handle it if I left. Not with so many of my brothers and sisters still so young. That's assuming I can *find* a job. I had to quit at Phifers."

"What?" Roberto sounded stunned.

"Yeah, last Thursday night. Ol' man Phifer wanted me to work on the Saturday of the big game. So I quit. I didn't want to miss what we've worked all year for. I mean, what was I supposed to do?"

Roberto slapped him on the shoulder. "Brother . . . am I ever glad you made the right choice."

The three boys stopped when they reached their lockers. Glen absentmindedly spun the dial of his combination while he thought. Finally he blurted out, "It's not fair. With your grades and record, you could probably go to any school you want, DT. Why should you be the one to sacrifice everything to take care of your family? Isn't Laurie old enough to—"

"Don't even talk about her," David said.

"I could talk some sense into that brat," Glen bragged. "Just say the word."

David snorted, "Ha. She'd probably beat you up."

Roberto pulled his letterman sweater off and

hung it in his locker. Reaching for his books, he turned to Glen. "What about you, Scraps?"

"What about what?"

"What're you gonna be doing—I mean, now that the season's over—what about next year? We never really thought much past this season. Any colleges interested in you?"

"Nah. No time for that . . . 'til now." Glen fidgeted and smiled. "I gotta admit, though . . . the thought of southern California in the winter seems pretty good to me. There's a reason why they have so many good teams down there. They can play ball all year round. They're not shoveling snow from November to April like we are."

David swallowed hard. "Sounds great."

"No doubt about it . . . Cal State Fullerton would be my choice. They've been to the College World Series every year lately, and . . . well . . . they're not known as 'Cal State Disneyland' for nothing. Sounds like fun."

David tried to find a bright side to his predicament. "Yeah, well, maybe in a couple of years, I could transfer down there with you. Or maybe"—his eyes grew bigger—"maybe we could both transfer down to Florida State and be closer to Disney*world*!"

The class bell clanged directly above their heads. The three boys jumped at the loudness.

"I guess that about wraps things up," Glen said. "I'll see you bozos later."

"If you're lucky," David shot back.

Roberto bumped forearms with David and laughed. David turned and walked down the hall. Roberto stood and watched for a second as his two best friends walked away in opposite directions.

"Hey, Mom. I'm home." Roberto barged into his house through the kitchen door. He eyed the chocolate cake on the counter with relish. "Can I cut into this cake?"

Rosa hustled into the kitchen and grabbed the knife out of Roberto's hand. "No, you may not! That's for our guest tonight."

Roberto appeared confused. "What guest? I didn't know we were having company."

Rosa whispered into his ear. "Mr. Cooper, from the University of Michigan, is out in the living room, Robbie. I've invited him to stay for dinner."

Roberto slapped his forehead. "Geez, Mom. I forgot all about him, since I didn't see him at school today. I didn't think that he'd just come straight here."

"He seems like a very nice man, Robbie. Straighten up a little and come out and join us. I called your father and he'll be home soon."

Roberto started to panic. "What should I wear? What should I say to him? I don't know—"

His mother stopped him in his tracks. "Just

settle down. You don't have to say or do anything special. Just relax and be polite."

"Right."

Roberto ducked up the stairs and into his room. He frantically riffled through his chest of drawers, looking for his favorite navy blue sweater. *Michigan's colors, at least,* he thought to himself as he checked his reflection in the mirror. *It'd probably be too much if I wore a gold shirt underneath.*

He dragged a comb through his hair and double-checked his appearance one last time. *This is as good as it gets. Let's go see what happens.*

When he entered the living room, Roberto was surprised to find his father had already joined Mr. Cooper. He heard them discussing career goals.

"Hi, Dad. You're home early." Roberto rolled his eyes as the words came out. *Geez, did that sound dumb*, he thought to himself.

"Roberto, come on in and meet Mr. Cooper."

The Michigan representative stood tall and took a step toward Roberto. "It's a pleasure to meet you, Roberto. I've been following your career for quite some time."

Roberto shook his outstretched hand. "It's nice to meet you, sir."

Cooper, middle aged, but just now starting to gray, sat back down in his chair. "That was one terrific ball game you pitched against East

High. Congratulations on the no-hitter—and the championship."

"Thanks. It's been an incredible year for our team. We all worked very hard."

"And I see that work has extended beyond the ball field to the classroom. You have excellent grades in all your subjects."

"Our coach has always insisted that we don't let baseball affect our schoolwork. He's pretty strict about everyone staying up in class."

Cooper tilted his head and smiled. "A three-point-eight-five in the solid subjects that you carry is more than staying up, Roberto. Combined with your score on the SAT tests . . . well . . . I guess you know why I'm here. We feel very strongly that you're the type of person the Wolverines are interested in."

Roberto's heart started pounding fast and hard in his chest. He quickly walked over to the sofa and sat down. Tongue-tied, Roberto was relieved his mother jumped into the conversation.

"Can I get you another cup of coffee, Mr. Cooper?"

"No, thank you, Mrs. Ramirez. But I would like to answer any of the questions you and your family might have about what Michigan has to offer. I think you'll find that we have an excellent program for Roberto."

Carlos nodded. "I'm sure you do, Mr. Cooper. You know, of course, that Roberto has always wanted to be a doctor."

"Yes."

Roberto watched his father closely. He knew his dad was not that concerned about baseball. Roberto wished he could tell him how much it meant to him.

Carlos continued, "So what exactly do you have in mind for my son?"

Folding his hands in his lap, Cooper stared directly into the elder Ramirez's eyes. "Our pre-med program takes a place second to none. It's a tough program; the wash-out rate is over eighty percent. But those who do stick it out are quickly accepted into the very best medical schools upon graduation. Of those who do go on to medical school from Michigan, seventy-five percent finish medical school and become doctors. That is an amazing percentage. If Roberto truly wants to become a doctor, he'll find no better place to find out than our school."

Roberto fought back an involuntary gulp in his throat.

Carlos proceeded to shock his son with his next question. "And what about the baseball program?"

Cooper went on to explain the Wolverine's success in the Big Ten and their fine tradition of winning sports. Roberto soaked it all up eagerly. The way Cooper spun the story, Roberto had no trouble seeing himself in the center of the picture of Michigan's moments of glory.

His daydream was interrupted when he heard Cooper question him. "I am assuming you'd like to continue your baseball career a little further, Roberto?"

"You'd better believe it, Mr. Cooper. I really love baseball. I don't think I would want to give it up right now."

Roberto's dad stared at him intently.

"Well, Roberto . . . and Mr. and Mrs. Ramirez." Cooper paused for effect and stood up to face them. "I want to tell you that I've come here to offer a full four-year scholarship to our school. It shows we have the utmost faith in Roberto and want him to succeed with us."

A hush fell over the Ramirez living room. The family sat frozen in their seats as Cooper's words rolled over and over again in their minds.

Roberto sat silently, trying to think of the right thing to say. His throat refused to swallow and his eyes grew heavy with moisture. Just as he was sure he was going to explode, his mother broke the tension.

"Why don't we all sit down and have dinner? I think we have a lot to talk about."

# ELEVEN

The next morning dawned overcast and muggy. David had scarcely slept the night before, and the uncomfortable heat wasn't the only reason.

At first, he'd watched the moonlit shadows dancing across his white ceiling while thinking about his future. In the afternoon, he, Glen, and Roberto were going to get together and listen to the sports reports of the major-league draft "just in case." But, as the hour grew later, he'd spent more and more time wondering when his sister Laurie was going to get in.

He flipped back the covers and crawled out of bed. He pulled on some sweat pants and headed for her room, determined to get to the bottom of the problem.

When David knocked and got no answer, he

figured she was just asleep, so he barged in. She wasn't there and her bed hadn't even been slept in. His eyes searched the room, frantically looking for some clue, but found none.

Racing back to his own bedroom, David threw on his sneakers and jetted down the stairs. He bolted out of the house in the direction of the Kings' house. Kathy King was Laurie's best friend and might be able to help.

David cut across the Kings' neatly manicured front lawn and bounded up the front steps. He rang the doorbell, then nervously shifted from one foot to the other as he waited. Finally, Mrs. King answered.

"David? What a surprise." She noticed the worried look on his face. "Is there something wrong?"

"Is Laurie here, Mrs. King? I need to talk to her."

"Well, I honestly don't know. I don't think so. . . ." She turned and yelled up the entry stairwell, "Kathy!"

She turned back to David. "Come on in, David. I didn't mean to keep you standing outside."

Kathy King skip-stepped down the stairs and seemed startled when she spotted David. He didn't wait for her to greet him.

"Kathy, is Laurie here?" he blurted out.

"No . . . not right now," she replied hesitantly.

"Do you know where she is?" His voice betrayed his desperation. "She didn't come home last night."

Kathy seemed to be holding something back. "I . . . I'm not real sure." She stared down at the floor sheepishly. She started to divulge her secrets. "She was here last night, David."

Mrs. King looked stunned. "Kathy? Why didn't you tell me? What's going on around here?"

"Laurie said she needed to get away from her house and think. She was talking about running away and . . . just a bunch of crazy stuff, Mom. I thought it would be okay if she stayed so we could talk." Kathy nearly broke into tears.

"So what happened?" asked David.

"Nothing. We stayed up most of the night talking . . . you know. When I woke up this morning . . . she was gone."

David was angry. "Well, what did she say? What's she gonna do? Where'd she go?"

Kathy's voice was cracking as she spoke. "I don't know . . . I mean . . . I thought everything was okay. She seemed to be happier when we feel asleep. I thought she'd be here when I . . . I don't know where she could be if she's not home."

David rolled his head from side to side and ran his fingers through his hair. Totally confused, he looked at Mrs. King, and then Kathy. "I don't, either."


Roberto flopped down into the well-worn family-room sofa at Glen's house and nervously reached for a magazine. "What time does this stuff start?" he asked his host.

Flipping through the television channels, Glen stopped when he finally found ESPN. "It's probably already started, since it's an East Coast thing. I wonder where the heck Green is?"

Roberto glanced down at his watch. "I didn't think he'd be late for this. He seemed as excited as we did last night when I talked to him. Maybe I should give him a call. He might have over-slept."

Roberto didn't mention the visit from the University of Michigan to his friend. He wanted them both to be there when he told them.

Glen grabbed the cordless phone and threw it across the room at Roberto. "Do it! Let's find him and get this show on the road."

After punching in David's phone number, Roberto stared at the TV screen while he waited. Mrs. Green finally answered and explained to Roberto that David was not home. Roberto was even more puzzled when she told him that she didn't know where he was. Clicking down the receiver, he turned to Glen and shrugged.

"Maybe he's already on his way over. He'll probably show up any minute."

Glen gave a thumbs-up sign. "Right. No way he'll want to miss this."

The boys waited for a *Sports Center Update* to get the progress of the major-league draft. As time dragged on, they started to get concerned about David.

Glen brought a bowl of grapes down from the kitchen. Tossing them in the air and catching them in his mouth, he stopped and threw one at Roberto. "Hey, why don't you try David's house again?"

"Nah. He would've called if he was there. He's gotta be somewhere else."

"Okay . . . where?"

Roberto shrugged.

Glen stood up and started walking toward the door. He paced back and forth between rooms until he finally exploded. "Okay, okay, this is driving me nuts. Waiting around here is driving me nuts. Green's driving me nuts. I'm gonna go find him."

Roberto laughed and said, "There's no question about it . . . you *are* nuts! Where do ya think you're gonna go . . . he could be anywhere?"

"So, at least I'll be doing something. Sitting around here was a stupid idea. We're probably not gonna get selected, anyway. Let's go down to Eat Burger. . . . Maybe we'll run into him there."

Roberto jumped up from the couch. "Okay . . . leave a message for Green in case he shows his face. Then we're outta here!"

Eat Burger was still quiet before the first rush of lunchtime customers. Glen and Roberto walked in and had their pick of seats. They sat next to the huge front window so they could easily see anyone coming or going. When they ordered, they asked Lilian if she'd seen him, but she hadn't.

After they picked over an order of Eat Burger deluxe platters and shakes, they became impatient.

"I swear that bozo Green doesn't know if he's coming or going sometimes. How could he screw up on a day like today?" Glen asked.

"Hey . . . I'm starting to think that there's something wrong somewhere. You gotta admit that DT isn't the type to miss anything, or, for that matter, even be late."

"So, what should we do next?"

Roberto shrugged his shoulders. "We might as well split up and see what we can find."

"You mean just wander around and try to find him?"

"No. Don't be stupid." Roberto was irritated by his friend's impatience. "There're a few places he might be, so why don't we hit those spots? You know . . . like his home. He might be back there now. Or maybe he went down to Phifer's to pick up his pay. Or the ball field or school or your house . . . I don't know. Let's just get outta here."

Glen jumped to his feet. "Okay. I'll check out Phifer's and then go to my house and wait for your call. You check out David's and the school and then let me know . . . okay?"

Roberto slapped him hard across the shoulders. "Got it. Catch ya later."

Roberto jogged the five blocks to David's house in a few short minutes. He smacked the doorbell and rapped twice on the door.

When no one answered, he peered through the glass panes next to the door and saw no lights or movement in the house. Disappointed, he skipped down the stairs of the front porch and headed off toward Rosemont High.

The seniors had already finished school, but there were still eight days left for the rest of the students. Roberto couldn't think of any reason why David would be at school but felt compelled to check it out anyway.

When he entered the hallways and strolled past his old locker, Roberto felt goose bumps forming. He knew, now more than ever, that he was going to miss what he had enjoyed so much for four years.

As he wandered down the long corridors, he suddenly realized that Coach La Russo's office was the logical place to look. He spun around, took a right-hand turn down the hall, and headed for the gymnasium.

Roberto spotted Coach La Russo through the window of his office. La Russo noticed him at the same moment and waved him in with a huge smile.

"Hey, Ramirez, good to see you."

"Good to see you, too, Coach."

"Congratulations, too. I heard the good news."

Roberto's face squinched up in puzzlement. "What news?"

"Michigan? Four-year ride? Does any of this ring a bell with you?"

Roberto laughed. "Geez. I did forget about that for a second. How did you know?"

La Russo puffed up his chest and leaned back in his chair. "Do you honestly think that something like that gets done without my knowledge? Let me fill you in, Magic—just in case you didn't learn anything during your four years here. I knew about that scholarship before you did."

"But I just talked to him. . . ."

"Yeah, and he just talked to me before he went to your house. Do you think he'd make a move without my input?"

Roberto put his hand out across the desk. "Thanks for all you've done, Coach. And not just with the scholarship, I mean."

La Russo grabbed the outstretched hand and shook it vigorously. "Hey, I'll never forget you, Magic. You're one of the greatest ones I've ever had the pleasure to work with. Good luck at Michigan and all through your life."

Roberto bowed his head. Then he jerked back upright and said, "Wait a minute. This sounds like you're saying good-bye. Don't think you've seen the end of me, Coach. 'Cause I plan on coming back here and bugging you every chance I get."

"That'd be great, Ramirez. I'd love to see it."

"You will." Roberto turned serious and remembered the original reason for his visit. "In fact, I was wondering if Dave Green's been over to see you today?"

"Nope. Why? Is he missing in action or something?"

"Sort of. He was supposed to meet Scrapper and me this morning, and we haven't been able to find him all day. We're starting to get a little nervous about it."

The conversation was abruptly interrupted by the harsh ring of the telephone. La Russo quickly grabbed the receiver, trying to stop a second attack of the blaring noise.

"La Russo," he answered. "Yes, Walt, how the hell are ya?"

Roberto sat down in the chair opposite Coach La Russo's desk. A knot formed in his throat and he suddenly had difficulty breathing. He didn't know why.

Coach La Russo's eyes suddenly focused on Roberto. "Yes. As a matter of fact, I happen to know exactly where he is."

Roberto's heart started beating in double time. He stared into his former coach's face and nervously waited for some word.

La Russo started laughing and joking with the voice on the other end of the line. "That's gonna be interesting, all right, Walt. But it's a problem that I'm sure he'll find the right answer to. Don't worry about it."

Roberto felt the air rush out of his lungs. He suddenly felt that the conversation no longer was about him. He didn't know if he was relieved or disappointed, but the indecision only lasted a moment.

"He's sitting right here," Coach La Russo said. "Do you want to talk to him?"

Roberto gasped.

"Ramirez . . . it's Roy Palumbis of the Dodgers. He'd like to have a word with you." The smile on La Russo's face was a mile wide.

"Me?" was all Roberto could utter.

"Well, he's already talked to me and you're the only one left in the room."

Roberto reached for the receiver and almost dropped it on the desk during the exchange. "Hello," he meekly answered.

"Yes. I remember you, Mr. Palumbis. . . . Uh-huh . . . Yes. . . ." Suddenly the worry on Roberto's face was replaced with an expression of shocked disbelief, quickly followed by uncontrolled, wild-eyed joy.

"You betcha I would. I'd give it a lot of thought!"

La Russo sat across from his ace pitcher with a satisfied smirk on his face.

Roberto nodded his head as he continued to speak on the phone. "You'd better believe it. I-I-I don't know what to tell you, Mr. Palumbis. . . .

Okay . . . 'Bye . . . Wait. Thanks a lot—thanks a million."

Roberto threw the phone back down in its cradle. He threw his hands up in the air and jumped straight out of his chair. "I can't believe it!"

La Russo stood and put his hands on the desk. Leaning forward, he said, "You'd better start believing it, kid. It's for real."

Roberto wanted to run out of the room. He wanted to leap as high as he could leap. He wanted to run to his house and tell everyone in his family. He wanted to find his two friends immediately and tell them the unbelievable news. He stood frozen in his tracks for a second, not knowing what to do first.

Coach La Russo put his arm around Roberto's shoulder. "Slow down for just a minute, Ace. Let it soak in for a second before you go off half-cocked. Besides, I want to enjoy this for a second myself. After all, it's not every day that a guy's lucky enough to have been the coach of the *number-one draft pick* of the Los Angeles Dodgers!"

Hearing the words out loud almost knocked Roberto to the ground. He said them to himself one more time, trying to convince himself it was really true. "Number-one draft pick of the Los Angeles Dodgers!"

# TWELVE

After a quick stop at Phifer's, with no success in finding David, Glen returned home. Flinging open the front door in disgust, he yelled out, "Green? You here?"

Receiving no answer, he made his way through the kitchen and toward the family room. As he grabbed an apple off the kitchen counter, he heard his father talking on the phone.

"I don't think you'll be disappointed. He's well worth your consideration."

Glen started to leave the room, but his father waved him back. Hearing only one side of the conversation, Glen knew nothing about what was happening.

His father ended the call by saying, "Thanks

again, John. He'll be thrilled to hear from you."

When the phone was put down, Glen impatiently asked his father, "Have you heard from DT at all?"

"Dave Green can wait. We've got more important things to discuss."

"Like what?"

"Like a chance to play professional ball."

The younger Mitchell didn't even look at his father. "What're you talking about?"

"I just talked to John Waters of the Phillies. I've convinced him that you deserve a shot, and they're going to take you in the second round. There's a pitcher in Florida they've got their heart set on in the first round, but they're gonna take you second. Isn't that great?"

Glen looked at his dad in surprise and then disgust. He turned and started to walk out of the room.

"Hey . . . where do you think your going?"

"Outta here."

"I thought you 'd be happy. Haven't we talked a million times about you playing pro ball someday?"

Glen stood silently with his head down. "Yeah. At least a million."

"So what's the problem?"

Glen yelled at his father. "Did you ever think that maybe I don't want or need your help?"

Joe Mitchell stepped backward and leaned against the wall. "And what's wrong with getting a little help? Don't think that it's easy out in the real world. What you know and what you can do only takes you so far. Sometimes it's *who* you know that can make or break a deal."

"And you know all the right people, right?"

"I didn't spend fifteen years kicking around the country without learning a few things and meeting a few key people. And what the hell's wrong with wanting my own son to get a chance?"

"Maybe, just maybe, I could have made it on my own. Did you ever think of that?"

"I only want the best for you, Glen."

Glen started to stomp out of the room. "Then just leave me alone." He stopped and shouted back, "And you can call the Phillies and tell them to drop dead. I wouldn't want to play in their organization."

The argument was abruptly interrupted by the phone. Glen started walking back into the room. "That's for me. It's Magic."

Joe Mitchell picked up the cordless phone and threw it toward his son. "Take it."

Pulling up the antennae, Glen flipped the phone on. "Hello, Mitchell residence . . . Yes, this is Glen."

Glen listened intently to the voice on the other end. He couldn't believe his own ears. He stood stock-still, his eyes starting to glaze over.

Joe Mitchell could tell something was up and he couldn't stand the suspense. "Who is it?" he whispered.

Glen pretended not to hear him.

His father poked him in the ribs. "What's going on? Who's on the phone?"

Glen threw his shoulders back and chest out. "It's WGN radio."

"Well . . . what do they want?"

"Hold on just a moment, please," Glen said as he covered the mouthpiece of the phone. A broad smile creased his face. "WGN radio wants to get my reaction to being the *first*-round draft choice of the Chicago White Sox."

Joe Mitchell started to smile. "Great, Glen!"

Turning his attention back to the phone, Glen answered several more questions before finally excusing himself from the call. His excitement was bubbling over and he couldn't contain himself any longer.

When he finally hung up, he turned and shouted to the world, "*First-round draft choice!*"

He then remembered his friends. "I can't wait to tell DT and Magic!"

Joe Mitchell grabbed his son by the arm. "I'm very proud of you son. I hope you know that."

Glen nodded his head. "I know, Dad." He clutched the phone in his hand and started punching in numbers. "Now for the tricky part. Finding them to tell them!"

The Ramirez household was in an uproar. When Roberto raced home and told them the news, his mother burst into tears and smothered him with hugs. Carlos had raced home after a frantic phone call and shared in the bedlam engulfing their home.

The phone rang off the hook as newspaper, radio, and television people tried to get the firsthand story on Roberto's selection.

Trying to break away from the bedlam, Roberto wanted to call Glen and share the excitement with him. He still hadn't heard from Dave Green.

"Mom, can you hold some of these people off while I try to call Glen?"

"I'll try, honey. But they all want you to say something."

"I will . . . I will. I just want to call Glen and tell him and see if he's heard from David."

Just as he found the phone to make his call, one more person barged into the house and yelled out over the noisy crowd. "Hey, Magic, what's going on around here?"

Roberto searched through the crowd until he spotted the source of the familiar voice. "Scrap! You're here!"

"Like everyone else in Rosemont," Glen said, elbowing his way to his friend. "I've been trying to call, but couldn't get through."

"I was just gonna call you. As if you couldn't guess, something big happened. I got drafted by the Dodgers!"

Scrapper reached his buddy and clutched his neck with a free hand. "That's super. That really makes things great."

Roberto could see the sparkle in Glen's eye. "What's that supposed to mean?"

"Hey . . . you're not the only one who's a celebrity."

"You mean . . ."

"Yep. White Sox . . . first round." A huge smile filled Glen's face.

"All right! Outta sight. This is unbelievable!"

The Rosemont stars smashed forearms above their heads.

Roberto shook his head again and screamed out, "This is absolutely unbelievable!"

The media crowd that filled the house recognized Glen and approached both boys. The questions were called out by dozens of people all at the same time.

"How does it feel to get drafted by the major leagues?" "Are you happy with the teams that selected you?" "What are your plans?" "Are you going to sign?" "Have you talked to DT Green yet?" "How does he feel about the Red Sox?"

Glen pointed toward the last voice. "What was that? What did you say about Green?"

"Haven't you boys heard? Green was selected by the Boston Red Sox—first round."

Glen and Roberto let out a whoop. "All right!"

The two boys both looked at each other at the same instant. "But where the heck is he?" they asked.

The questions continued for over an hour as every detail of the boys thoughts, hopes, and dreams were discussed. By the time the last reporter was ready to leave, Roberto and Glen were exhausted.

They collapsed on the Ramirezes' living room sofa and took a deep breath.

Glen jumped back to his feet. "Hey. If DT's been gone since this morning, he probably doesn't even know he's been drafted. We got to find him to tell him the good news."

Roberto pulled himself up and said, "Yeah. Come on! Let's go!"

As they bounded down the front walkway, they watched Coach La Russo's bright red Ford slowly pull up to the curb and stop.

A second later, David swung open the passenger side and climbed out. A big grin covered his face.

"Hey, guys, what's happening?"

Roberto and Glen looked at each other. They didn't know where to start.

Coach La Russo spoke before they could. "Ramirez told me you guys were concerned about Green here. So, I checked around and found him. Had to tell him the news, too."

Glen, David, and Roberto bumped forearms and shouted, "All right, Coach!"

Glen gave David a playful shove. "Now tell us. Where the heck have you been hiding?"

David told them the whole story about his missing sister. He had searched all over town for her and then remembered how she used to like to go to Observatory Rock. He found her there and spent the day trying to talk some sense into her.

"I guess I finally got through," he said. "She's decided to get a part-time job after school and start helping out at home. She's even gonna try and be nice to my mother for a change."

"That's super. It looks like everything is falling into place," Roberto said.

Glen shook his head from side to side. "Only one thing puzzles me."

"What?" David said.

"I don't know what got into the Red Sox. Wasting a draft pick like that."

David threw a headlock around Scrapper and wrestled him to the ground. "Wasted, huh? We'll see who spends their entire professional baseball career on an A-club bench. The only way you'll ever see Comiskey Park is if you buy a ticket!"

Roberto jumped on top of the pile. "Don't worry. When you guys want to see some real ball, I'll get you into Dodgers Stadium, half price." Mitchell and Green jumped on him for that.

"I'm leaving," Coach La Russo said, laughing. "It's getting too deep around here for us short people. Congratulations, guys. Stay in touch."

The three Rosemont aces scrambled to their feet and waved to their coach, yelling, "Thanks!" as he drove off down the street.

David, Roberto, and Glen all glanced at each other. There were a million things to say, but no place to start. The uncomfortable silence was broken when Glen smacked his friends on the back and said, "The field in half an hour."

The other two boys gave a thumbs-up and all three friends ran off in different directions. Twenty minutes later, they were back together again . . . on the Rosemont Park baseball diamond.

David threw a high, towering fly ball that Glen carefully circled under. The ball popped loudly into his well-worn glove as he made the grab.

"Can't you throw it any higher than that?" he yelled out as he flung a rifle shot back toward David.

"I could, but you'd never find it." David flipped a lazy grounder in the direction of Roberto.

"Hey, I'm a pitcher, not a shortstop," Roberto said, scooping up the ball and firing it to Glen.

The trio relaxed, as they had done a thousand times before, by flipping the ball around the horn to each other in a game of catch. The tensions, dramas, and anxieties of the day all seemed to melt away with the simple return to basics: throwing and catching a ball.

Glen yelled out to his friends, "Well? What's the story? You guys gonna sign or what?" It was a question that no one needed to ask him.

"I can't afford not to," shouted David, throwing another fly ball to Roberto. "The signing bonus will go a long way to giving my mom some financial security for the first time. We could pay off the house, and I'd still have me a nice chunk of change."

Roberto caught the ball and threw a grounder toward Glen. "Yeah. They're talking about paying for my college during the off-season. Plus, with what I'd get for signing, I could pay my way to any school if the majors don't pan out. I can't lose."

Glen scrambled for the ball and whipped one back to Green. "Well, it's no secret I've always wanted to play pro ball. It's no tough decision for me."

He walked toward his two best friends and offered a high-five. The three of them met in a loud hand slap. "I guess that makes it official. From now on, we're the *Rookies*!"

Follow our ROOKIES as they burn up the turf in the minor leagues in the next action-packed book . . .

ROOKIES #2: Squeeze Play

FIC
FRE

Freeman, Mark

Play Ball!